Four Horsemen

Katie Dunn

Titles by Katie Dunn

Ancient Elements

Myth Blessed

Four Horsemen

Sapphire Sparks

<u>Skor Stone Trilogy</u>
Pirates from Under
Prince of Shayd

Chapter 1

A Nittany lion wearing a striped scarf danced around the quad in the center of the University. Booths were set up across the lawn and the lion encouraged people to approach the tables. Tons of Freshmen walked around with folders, lanyards, and suitcases causing the quad to be crowded. Some of them posed in front of the mascot and took selfies, which blocked the walkway. Others crowded around tables or shuffled about exploring their new home. The mascot costume weirded me out, so I made sure to avoid it and blended into the crowd as I searched for a check-in booth.

Penn State University was my first choice in colleges, and I had been super excited last year to open the envelope and see my acceptance letter. However, now that I was there, nerves twisted my stomach. I finally found the check-in booth and rushed over before the line got longer. Thankfully, it wasn't a long wait.

"Hello, welcome to Penn State. What's your name?" A young woman asked as she beamed at me from the other side of the table.

I wondered if she was paid to be there or volunteered. "Ophelia Bronson." I cringed at the use of my first name. Ophelia sounded like an old lady name or a delicate flower, both of which I was not.

The woman looked down at her checklist of Freshmen names. "Ah, Engineering, how fun," she said, studying my information. "You are going to be in the West Residence Halls, which fortunately for you are near here." The woman handed over a map, a key, and a Nittany lion sticker. "Go Nittany Lions!" She cheered enthusiastically.

I pumped a fist half-heartedly in the air and gave a pathetic cheer in return. Well, it looked like cheerleading was off the table.

I grabbed the stuff she held and left the table so the person behind me could check in. I glanced down at the map and found the West Residence Halls. Once I got my bearings on where I was, I followed the map to my new home. I didn't have any luggage other than a backpack with me, my parents promising to send my stuff soon, so I was able to get around campus free of heavy burdens.

The woman was right when she said it was near the quad. I barely had to walk that far to reach the West Residence Halls. Feeling a sense of excitement about new beginnings, I reached out and yanked on the door. Then I yanked again. The door rattled but refused to open. I peered inside but the windows were dark preventing me from seeing much. I sighed in frustration and looked for a way in. A small button and speaker near the door caught my attention so I stalked over to it and jabbed the button with a bit of annoyance.

The speaker crackled then a male voice sounded, "West Residence Halls, how can I help you?"

I looked around for a phone or something to speak into, but the speaker was the only thing in sight. I leaned toward it and raised my voice a little in case they couldn't hear outside voices very well. "My dorm is inside but I don't have a way in."

"Where is your student ID?" the voice asked.

I frowned and patted myself down even though I knew I didn't have one. "I don't have one yet, I am a Freshman."

"You need an ID to enter." The speaker crackling cut off making me assume the person stopped listening.

I pressed the button again and the crackling of the speaker sounded again. "West Residence Halls, how can I help you?"

"Hi, uh, my room is 102 but I don't have an ID to get in." I held up my room key that the enthusiastic check in lady gave me as if the speaker guy could see it.

"You need an ID to enter." The cackling shut off again and I kicked the wall in frustration.

He could have at least told me how to go about getting one.

I fumed in annoyance and yanked at the doors again, hoping they would open for me despite not having an ID. When they continued to stay closed, I stomped my foot, feeling childish but I didn't care. I leaned against the brick wall and crossed my arms. The next time someone came in or out, I would sneak in.

It didn't take long until the doors opened, and a couple of people walked out deep in conversation. I sidled passed them and slipped inside, feeling triumphant and wanting to rub it in speaker boy's face. Instead, I glanced down at the number on my key, even though I already knew it, and went to search for room 102.

Thankfully, it was on the first floor, so it didn't take me long to find my room. I used the key in my hand to open the door to my new life. Light shown in through a window opposite the door, highlighting two sets of bunk beds situated against opposite walls. The bottom part of the bunk beds hid desks instead of a bed, efficiently opening the space of the room a little more.

A female voice startled me from the right side of the room. "You can move the desk and lower the bed if you want."

I hadn't noticed someone sitting under one of the beds at the desk. The woman stood up and reached out a hand to me. She had dark skin and ultra-curly brown hair. Her brownish gold eyes shown with kindness and intelligence.

"I'm Shawna, Engineering major" she introduced.

I didn't want to continue standing there like an idiot who didn't realize she would have a roommate, even though that's exactly who I was. I reached forward and shook her hand, "You can call me Phi. I'm also an Engineering major."

Shawna smiled at me and nodded. We fell into an awkward silence, neither of us knowing what to say next. I hadn't always been socially awkward. I used to be outgoing and friendly and always knew just the thing to say. However, life happened, I became withdrawn and now my friends were mainly machines and oil grease. This year, though, I was determined to make at least one real friend.

"Do you need any help unpacking?" Shawna asked, looking around for my luggage.

I shook my head and waved her offer away. "I don't have anything right now except for my backpack. I was going to go shopping later to pick up some stuff."

Shawna's eyes lit up. "I will come with you. I need a few things as well."

I gave her a small smile, happy that she would want to tag along even though it was something that would probably be boring for anyone involved. We fell into silence again. I was sure I would get better at talking to people at some point, but maybe not today. I placed my map and backpack on my desk and fiddled with my red beaded Hawaiian bracelet nervously. It was a weird tic I picked up over the last year.

Shawna somehow knew what to do though. She grabbed her keys and waved at me to follow her. "Let's go to the orientation assembly."

I breathed a sigh of relief. Going outside and doing something sounded better than hanging around an empty room. I followed her out and let her lead us to wherever the orientation was being held. I had forgotten to grab my map, so I hoped she knew where we were going.

We ended up back over at the main quad area where Freshmen continued walking around trying to check-in and see all the new sights. The same Nittany lion danced around the people still and I cringed at its behavior. I would never want to have that job. Orientation was apparently in the Schwab Auditorium which was across the lawn from the student Union. Noise and people invaded my senses inside the auditorium. I was surprised to see the place was nearly packed despite all the people still outside. We grabbed seats near the back and waited for the orientation to start.

"So where are you from?" Shawna asked, breaking the ice once again.

I hesitated, not really wanting to say but there was no reason for me to be secretive. "Philadelphia. You?"

"Chicago," Shawna beamed. "I've always wanted to live in Pennsylvania and figured this University was a good way for that to happen." She looked around as she held out her hands to encompass the auditorium and Penn State. Then she turned to me. "Is your name Phi due to you living in Philadelphia?"

I cringed. Many people believed that was the reason for my name Phi. That or sorority reasons. "No, it's because Ophelia doesn't really suit me. Pennsylvania is a neat place to live, good choice." I started fidgeting with the Hawaiian bracelet on my wrist again, feeling nervous about talking to someone about my life.

"So, what made you add a white streak to your hair?" Shawna asked side blinding me with the topic change.

My hand jerked up to my hair and grabbed the white streak that ran through the dark locks. The stupid streak that had appeared a year ago after my brother's…after he left. I had tried dyeing it and cutting it off, but it always reappeared, so now I just lived with it. People thought I added it on purpose especially since natural white streaks at a young age were rare. It was easier to let them think that.

"Phi?" Shawna asked, touching my shoulder to get my attention.

I dropped my hair and stared at her questioningly. I forgot what she asked.

"Why did you add a white streak?" She repeated. Her brows drew down into a small frown.

Oh no. I was being weird. I've known her for less than an hour now and I was already ruining what could be my first friendship since last year.

I shook my head and dropped my gaze. "It looks cool," I finally answered. I didn't like telling people it was natural because that would raise more questions and those led to tears and…I just didn't like talking about it.

"Oh my God," Shawna grabbed my arm, jolting me out of my thoughts, and leaned closer to me. "Look at the guys that just walked in. They're gorgeous," she shouted in a whisper.

Shawna didn't seem fazed by my weird behavior or vague answers. I sighed in relief and chuckled at my new roommates' energy and frequent topic changes. If that was how everyday would be, I would get exhausted. I looked over to the door to see who she was talking about and froze.

How the hell did they find me? Of course, they could have been there because it was an amazing University, but I had a niggling feeling it was because I attended. I slid down in my seat to avoid their notice and watched as they continued further into the room to sit a few rows in front of us. This was just great. I had been avoiding them for a year now and thought I had driven them off for good when I destroyed their motorcycles. I remembered their stricken looks when their babies went up in flames. I had not been surprised when they stopped coming around after that.

"You know them?" Shawna whispered excitedly.

When she saw my scowl, she glanced at the guys with her head tilted in curiosity. "Who are they?"

I had to swallow a knot in my throat and push back the tears that stung my eyes before I could answer. "That's Kaden," I told her, pointing to the one with russet brown hair and orange highlights. If he were facing us, I knew we would be able to see his forest green eyes and dimples as he smiled. I pointed to the one with obsidian black hair and brown jacket sitting next to him. "That one is Trevor."

I moved my finger to point to the last one. He had the softest looking brown hair and I knew if he turned around his eyes would be a piercing hazel-brown and he would have a beard recently shaven, but its shadow would still show. "That's Liam, the leader of the group." I turned to my roommate with concern. "Watch out around them, they are not good guys."

I don't know why, but that seemed to intrigue her even more. I sighed and shook my head hoping she would heed my warning. She didn't get to ask any more questions, because a tall, dark, bald man in a suit walked up to the podium and welcomed the new Freshman class of Penn State University.

He went over the history of the school, important tips for us to know and how vital signing up for clubs was when we were still Freshmen. Most of it went in one ear and out the other because I couldn't stop staring at the back of the heads of the three guys I wanted to see the least in the world. I didn't even realize the orientation ended until Shawna tapped my arm and ushered me out of my seat so we wouldn't hold up the row. As soon as I was up, I moved quickly to the door and out of the auditorium, then I kept walking not waiting to see if Shawna was behind me. All I wanted to do was get far away. Shawna caught up to me in the quad, and I relaxed a bit knowing the crowd would help me blend in.

"I know it's none of my business, but you seem to have real issues with them. You have been on edge ever since they got here." Shawna hesitated and leaned closer. "Did they hurt you?"

I shook my head vehemently and waved her statement away. "No, nothing like that. They're just guys from back home."

I know that cleared nothing up, but I had only known Shawna for an hour. I wasn't quite ready to spill my guts about my life. Thankfully she let it drop and instead looped her arm through mine, pulling me away from the quad to the outskirts of campus.

"C'mon, let's go shopping," Shawna suggested, changing the subject.

I cringed at the idea of shopping, but it was that or sleep on a plain mattress and wear the same three sets of clothes for the rest of my life. The closest store to our dorm was Wal-Mart, and while I preferred to support local businesses, it was convenient. Shawna had a great time helping me pick out bedding and clothes. I couldn't care less what color my bedsheets were but since she continued asking, I went with some pale green sheets and a dark green comforter. On our way out we passed by the bikes and I couldn't help but stop and stare. Having a bike to get around campus would be nice, plus it would remind me of my bike back home. I browsed the various types and went with a pale colored bike with a basket.

Shawna smirked at my choice but said nothing. I understood her smirk. Most people looked at me and thought punk or street rat since I worked with machines and avoided people. They thought I was someone who liked ripped jeans, black t-shirts, rock music, and motorcycles. The black t-shirts may be true but the rest of it was not really my style. I mean who thought ripped jeans were stylish? It just didn't make sense. I wheeled the bike and the rest of my belongings to check out and purchased them.

Once we got all my stuff back to the dorm, Shawna guided me to the bookstore and administration building to get my books and ID. Thank goodness I had her to help me get around because I would have gotten lost at least five times. Our last stop was the on-campus dining area and my stomach grumbled in anticipation. The atmosphere inside almost felt like a buffet where we had to go to the various sections to get our food and could eat as much as we wanted while we were there.

"I heard they have a variety of food like pasta, sandwiches, pizza, and grilled items." As Shawna continued listing food types her voice got higher in excitement. Then she rushed off to fill her plate.

I chuckled at her enthusiasm for food and figured it would be a good friendship after all. I ended up getting a club sandwich, some veggies, and root beer. Shawna was already seated with her hamburger and pasta near the back of the dining area, so I walked back there and joined her. We received nineteen meals per week and I already knew we would be spending most of them here. If it was all you can eat, then why not?

I was only halfway through my food when a hulking figure stood at the head of the table casting his shadow over us. I knew I hadn't seen the last of them, but I never expected for one of them to stop by while I was eating. I looked up and saw dimples flash at us.

"Hey, Phi, long time no see," Kaden waved and without an invitation he sat down next to Shawna forcing her to move over.

Shawna stared at him with wide eyes and looked him up and down with intrigue. Kaden noticed and turned to her with an open hand. "Hi, I'm Kaden Hallahan, and you are?"

Shawna put her hand in his, holding it a second longer than necessary for a greeting. "Shawna Matthews."

He gave her a hypnotizing smile that I knew could melt any girl's heart. He had used it many times on the girls in high school, but he would not flirt with my new friend. I kicked him under the table causing him to frown and look back at me. I glared at him, trying to tell him he was not welcome, but he only chuckled and leaned his elbows on the table, resting his chin on his hands. His green eyes pierced my own pale ones and a flash of danger sparked in their depths, but it was gone as quick as it came.

Kaden stood up and smiled at both of us. "See you around Phi." He knocked on the table in goodbye and left us sitting there with the rest of our food. Suddenly I was no longer hungry.

"I like him, he seems nice," Shawna commented as she stared at his retreating behind.

If only she knew how dangerous he could be. How dangerous they all could be.

Chapter 2

I found myself having to get up early for my first set of classes and groaned. College was supposed to eliminate the early mornings, but Freshmen didn't get that luxury I supposed. I dragged myself out of bed and walked over to our little sink near the door and brushed my teeth and fixed my hair before leaving the room to go to the bathroom that was thankfully only three doors down. I hated how it was a communal bathroom, but I figured it was better than having to clean my own.

Once I was ready, I grabbed my backpack, shoved a couple of notebooks in and raced out of the room. Shawna was already gone, being a morning person, she had scheduled a 6am Yoga class and got up two hours ago. I didn't have time to stop by the dining hall for breakfast, so I raced by it on my new bike and reached the Math building. Unfortunately, I had to take Math and English as a Freshman, so I put those as my first two classes to get them out of the way. I really just wanted to get right into my Engineering classes but basics first.

I arrived ten minutes before class and the large room only had a few seats left. I chose a seat near the door to make a quick getaway afterward and put my bag under my seat, deciding not to pull out a notebook because it would probably be a day of getting-to-know-you stuff. A body fell into the seat beside me, but I didn't look to see who it was. I didn't feel like making small talk with anyone, especially in the morning since I was not fully awake yet.

"Hello, Phi," a deep grumbly voice greeted me from my right.

I closed my eyes, hoping I imagined the voice but when I opened them and looked over, Trevor stared back with his deep blue eyes. I pursed my lips and gave him a small wave before crossing my arms and turning back to the front. That was two of them in less than twenty-four hours. I had a bad feeling I would be seeing them more often than I wished.

"Why are you in this class? I would have thought you would have tested out," I grumbled, still refusing to look at him.

Trevor was an amazing mathematician and had always talked about going to school to study Math and Economics. I would have expected him to be starting out in a 300-level class rather than the beginner course.

I saw him shrug from the corner of my eye, but he didn't say anything more. Trevor had always been a quiet guy and he had a boyish charm about him that attracted all kinds of girls, but I knew underneath all that he could be hella dangerous.

Three guys during junior year in high school accidentally bumped into him at lunch once causing his tray of food to crash to the floor and splash cheese ravioli everywhere, including all over Trevor. Both the splatter and what followed was not a pretty sight. I shuddered at the memory.

I heard him unwrap something then a moment later a peanut butter cracker appeared in front of me. Trevor didn't say anything, just laid it down in front of me and started munching on one of his own. Usually I would not accept anything from him, but I was hungry. I quickly snatched up the cracker and stuffed the whole thing in my mouth, feeling like a chipmunk with stuffed cheeks as I chewed. Trevor chuckled and continued eating, sliding me another one when I finished the first. Begrudgingly, I picked it up and held it like it was a precious item.

Food was heaven.

The professor walked in, announcing himself to the class, causing everyone to quiet down. He continued by spending the whole class period explaining his course, introducing himself and forcing us to play a game. When it got to the game, I shrank down feeling nervous about people knowing something about me. It was two truths and a lie and thankfully he started at the other end of class. I racked my brain trying to think of something to say. My truths could be that I was from Philadelphia and I liked working on machines. The lie was harder because that required me to think of something that was near truth in order to fool people. However, I didn't need to put so much effort into such a silly game so I just picked three random things and sat back to wait for my turn.

Trevor rumbled next to me making me look up to see the cause. The professor looked straight at him, but Trevor stayed quiet.

"Why don't you tell us your name," the professor suggested.

Trevor glared at him before answering, "Trevor Jackson."

The professor waited for him to say more but when Trevor didn't continue, he prompted, "What are your two truths and lie?"

Trevor scowled and crossed his arms. He didn't want to do that activity any more than I did. The whole class continued staring until finally Trevor ground out, "I ride a motorcycle, I have two brothers, and I have three tattoos."

The professor smiled and turned to the class to have them try and figure out his lie. I glanced at him, knowing he technically spoke two lies and a truth. He did have a motorcycle, well I assumed he replaced the one I burnt down, but he only had one tattoo and the two brothers he referred to were not truly related to him.

"Is your lie about your tattoos?" the professor asked still trying to get him engaged in the dumb game.

Trevor shrugged. "Sure."

It wasn't really an answer, but the professor decided to move on anyway. That meant it was my turn. I took a deep breath and calmed my trembling hands. I hated being the center of attention, too many eyes and judging stares.

"My name is Phi Bronson, and I am from Philadelphia, I like working on machines, and I have a brother." I decided to get it over with fast and not prolong the inevitable.

The professor tapped his chin thinking about my responses. A girl from the other side of class raised her hand and guessed that I was lying about working on machines. I shook my head making her frown.

"Are you lying about having a brother?" the professor guessed.

Tears sprung up and nearly fell. That hit me harder than I thought it would. Crying on my first day would be the icing on the cake of embarrassment. I pinched myself and forced the tears down, refusing to break down during my first week of college. I nodded and looked away to let the professor know he was done torturing me now and could move on. The professor called on a girl behind me, but I didn't hear anything she said, too focused on holding my emotions at bay. A hand settled on my arm and I looked up to see blue eyes shining with the same emotion. Trevor gave my arm a squeeze then pulled his hand back and continued to eat his crackers.

The professor called the end to class and I sprung up and rushed out, wanting to leave the Math building as fast as possible. I unlocked my bike, jumped on and raced to the Language Arts building not too far away. I really hoped that Math class had not set the mood I would be in for the rest of the day. I thought about calling my mom and telling her how I was feeling but knew she wouldn't be any help. My parents weren't really the comforting type these days.

Thanks to my speedy exit, I arrived fifteen minutes early, just in time to find a good seat in the back and calm my breathing. This class I could actually enjoy. I loved reading and didn't mind writing essays about interesting topics. Plus, I only had to take it for one semester then I would never have to see an English class again. I spun in my chair, fascinated by the fact that our desks were part of our chairs and could be rolled around. If I were more extroverted, I might have tried to convince someone to play bumper desks.

The professor walked in with a briefcase and started setting up near a podium at the front. He was much older than the Math professor, with white frizzy hair and a suit that had patches on the elbows. I smiled, instantly liking him.

Then my smile dropped when a tall, gorgeous, annoying and frustrating man walked through the door. You have got to be freaking kidding me. This theme that was going on was going to be the end of me if it continued. Liam stopped at the door and looked around, as if searching for someone. When his eyes landed on me, a slow grin spread over his face and his eyes narrowed. Out of all three of the guys, Liam Griffiths, was the most dangerous.

He was considered the King of our high school and got the reputation by conquering every club and sport in the place. He also had a habit of getting into fights.

He stalked toward the back of the room, causing my heart to race with panic. I nearly jumped up and ran out, but I was able to contain the urge. Liam stopped by my desk and stared hard into my eyes, smirking at me as if he knew how uncomfortable I was near him.

"Hello, High Phi," he said in a low, deep voice. He snatched a rolling desk nearby and pulled it over so he could sit next to me. This close I could see the stubble peeking through along his jaw and his more hazel than brown eyes shining with arrogance.

I grumbled at his use of my old nickname. When I was ten, I enjoyed using my name as a pun and went around asking people for high fives but instead of saying it like that I would say high phi. Liam liked making fun of me for it and started calling me High Phi.

"How have you been?" Liam asked in a smooth voice that felt like velvet across the ears.

He had his head propped up on his hand and stared at me with his constant half smile, made even more attractive by the stubble beard. He always seemed to be in on a joke that no one around knew about. Knowing him, he was probably up to something and that was what made him amused.

I ignored him, knowing if I said anything, he could use it against me later. The most innocent comment could be turned around and used as ammunition. I pulled out my phone and stared down at it, not focusing on it too much, but enough so I could ignore him. A piece of paper dropped onto my desk drawing my attention away from my phone. I stared at it, knowing it was from Liam but not wanting to pick it up. Curiosity got the best of me and I lowered my phone and grabbed the note, carefully opening it so only I could see what was inside.

What's your phone number?

I crumbled up the paper and threw it at Liam. "None of your business."

The last thing I needed was for him to have my number so he could bother me with tons of messages. I had made sure to change my number after I burned their motorcycles so that they could not reach me. Liam grinned at my response and leaned toward me.

"I got a new bike." He waited for me to react, but I gave him nothing.

By bike, he meant motorcycle and that did not surprise me. They loved motorcycles. Once upon a time I would have had one too, but that was all in the past. If he expected me to get mad about that or pale at the idea of it then he was wrong. Liam would not get a reaction out of me today. The professor called our attention and Liam sat back, deciding to leave me alone for the time being. Even though, I was facing the teacher, I couldn't help but watch Liam from the corner of my eye. He had the kind of presence that demanded attention. I glanced around the classroom and noticed more than a few curious glances in his direction. He would definitely have his share of interested ladies this year.

I gave a mental disgusted snort and focused back on the professor. He was outlining the course for us by going through his syllabus one detail at a time. The usual first day stuff. Thankfully he did not make us play an ice breaker and class was over before I knew it. As soon as he dismissed the class, I stood up, knocking my rolling seat back and dashed for the door. I only had twenty minutes to get to my next class, which was finally an Engineering class, but it happened to be back near my dorm, so I had to book it.

That and I really did not want to talk to Liam.

"Phi, wait," Liam called out.

I did the opposite and walked faster. I got to my bike and started to unlock it, but I didn't do it fast enough. Liam came to stand by me and grabbed my arm to stop me from leaving.

"Phi, we need to talk," Liam gave me an earnest gaze, the cockiness from before gone, and I deflated a little.

"Maybe next time." I sighed and shook off his arm. "I have to go to class." I hopped on my bike and gave him one last solemn glance before riding off to the Engineering building.

The Engineering building was packed, with students running around all over the place trying to get to their classes. I walked up to the second floor and entered the room I needed to be in. I had high hopes for Engineering Design and found myself sitting near the front rather than hiding in the back. A low squeal sounded and a girl with curly brown hair flew toward me.

"Yay, we have this class together," Shawna exclaimed and threw herself into a seat next to me.

I gave her a genuine smile, glad that I finally had a class with someone I enjoyed being around. The guys set me on edge, but I could relax around Shawna. The class was fantastic, although today it was mainly about introducing everyone but the plan for the semester sounded fun. There was an ice breaker but at least this time it only involved saying our name, major, and one thing about ourselves. By the end of class I was excited for the rest of the semester and planned on getting ahead in the work as soon as possible.

"What do you have next?" Shawna asked as we gathered our stuff and headed out of class.

I looked at my schedule and grinned. "Nothing until two." I was glad I had a couple hours until my next class. College may be great after all.

"My Religion Studies class is at one, but I could get a quick bite if you want to," Shawna suggested. "There is a great chicken wing place near here."

That sounded absolutely amazing. Hot wings were the bomb. I nodded enthusiastically and let her lead us there. It was in the same building as the on-campus dining hall but instead of turning left we went straight ahead until we came across a line in front of a mini wing take-out place. We ordered our food and sat at a table nearby. I opened my takeout box and inhaled the tangy aroma of buffalo sauce, my mouth immediately watering in response. Shawna chuckled at me and bit into her chicken sandwich.

I dipped some of my French fries in extra sauce and closed my eyes as the delicious flavor settled on my tongue. "This is officially my favorite food place."

We ate in silence for a while, well I did while Shawna chattered on about her morning classes, until we were scraping the bottom of the containers. I knew Shawna would have to go in a minute which meant I would have to find something to do for an hour.

"So, I'm not sure how you feel about parties," Shawna said slowly as she gathered her trash to throw away, "but there is one happening on Friday if you're interested." Shawna stared at me carefully, wondering what my answer would be.

She looked like she wanted me to say yes but as my friend wouldn't push it if I truly wished not to go. I had been to parties before in my Sophomore and Junior year of high school. About a year ago though, I quit going out completely and had turned into something of an introvert. I studied my friend's face and realized she was excited about the party. How she found out about one so fast, I had no idea. If anything, I could go just to hang out with her. I didn't need to drink or talk to others.

"Sure, sounds like it might be fun." I smiled at her excited squeal and had to catch myself from falling over when she launched herself from her seat to give me a hug. I laughed at her excitement and patted her back.

Shawna pulled back and shouldered her backpack. "Alright, girl, we will have to get you some kickass clothes before then. I gotta run, see you later."

I waved as she left, packing up my own things to leave and cleared the table for someone else. I was not looking forward to dressing up, but I knew Shawna would not let me go in jeans and a t-shirt. I tossed my trash away and started to leave but had to stop as I was suddenly blocked on all sides by three huge dudes.

"Are you stalking me?" I directed to Liam but cast my glare on all three.

They gave each other a look then shrugged at me. I gaped at their almost admission to stalking and crossed my arms.

"I have somewhere to be," I lied, hoping they would move and let me go on my merry way.

No such luck it seemed.

"We need to talk," Liam repeated his comment from earlier.

"Did you say you are going to the party on Friday?" Trevor asked with an accusatory tone.

My mouth dropped at his tone and the fact he heard me. "So, what if I am. Who do you guys think you are anyway? Stop stalking me." With that I pushed passed them and walked away as fast as I could without drawing attention.

It didn't matter. Everyone seemed to be looking at the guys, not even giving me a second glance. Thank God for that. I picked up my pace and got my bike unlocked before they caught up to me.

"You can't go. It's dangerous," Kaden said, putting his hand on my bike to stop me from leaving.

I guffawed. "Dangerous? The only danger to me is you three."

He visibly flinched at my words. I almost felt bad but didn't take it back. They were practically harassing me after all.

"Let go of my bike," I bit out.

Kaden held his hands up to show he meant no harm and I got on my bike, ready to ride off far away from them.

"You really shouldn't go to that party," Liam called out.

I ignored him and rode away. I was fuming by the time I reached my dorm. Who did they think they were? They weren't my brothers. I almost choked on a sob at the thought but let the anger push it away. If I had any doubts about attending the party, they were long gone by now. I was going to let Shawna dress me up and I was going to show them that they had no control over me.

Chapter 3

The week passed by in a blur. I was already up to my neck in homework and had spent every waking moment either focusing on classwork or avoiding the guys. Even though the work was piling up and we were already assigned projects, I thoroughly enjoyed it. College was my time to learn about what I wanted so I wouldn't complain about the work. However, it was Friday night now and I faced a whole new dilemma.

"Mini skirt or leggings?" Shawna asked, holding a jean skirt in one hand and a pair of pants in the other.

"For me or you?" I grimaced at both options. I preferred my legs covered but not restricted.

Shawna rolled her eyes and walked over to me, holding the skirt against my hips to see how it would look. I swatted it away, already determined that skirts would be the last option. Shawna put her hands on her hips and frowned at me.

"You are going to dress up with me if you are going to go." Shawna looked down at the carpet, suddenly serious. "Unless you don't want to go with me."

The fight left me at seeing my roommate's vulnerable expression. I had only known her for a week, but she already struck me as confident. Seeing her less than that shocked me.

"I am going, don't worry." I walked over to my closet and grabbed the skinny jeans in the far back. Shawna convinced me to buy them when we were shopping for my bedding and new clothes. "But I will be picking my own clothes."

Shawna's face brightened and she skipped to her closet and started tossing clothes on her bed. An hour later, we stood outside a large house on the outskirts of campus. Music boomed through the walls and college kids looking drunk already dotted the lawn leading up to the door. I clenched and unclenched my fists over and over nervously. This was the first time I had been to a party in a year and it was my first college one. Shawna gripped my hand and I swiveled my head to look at her in surprise. She looked as nervous as I was although her glittery pink eye shadow hid it well.

"Ready?" She asked, squeezing my hand.

I squeezed back and we both walked up the three steps to the door and pushed it open to face the chaos. The music got significantly louder when we entered the house and bodies crowded every room. We forced our way through the undulating masses to the kitchen where we found some reprieve and drinks. Shawna held her acquired cup of foul smelling liquid up to me and I cheered with her at our accomplishment of getting through the house unscathed.

"Ready?" Shawna shouted over the noise.

Instead of shouting back I tilted my head in confusion causing her to chuckle. She grabbed my shoulders and turned me around, pushing me back out into the crowd. I let her guide me even though I didn't want to dance. When she pushed me far enough, she came to stand in front of me and moved her hips to the music. I stood like a statue among the moving bodies, suddenly feeling self-conscious. I glanced around and was met with drunk revelry.

Shawna grabbed my hands and moved them up and down in an attempt to get me to dance. Seeing how happy and relaxed she was I decided to push all my worries aside and just have fun. College was about new beginnings and I would make the most of it. I followed her lead and lifted my hands above my head as I moved my hips to the music. At some point, after a song or two, we made our way back to the kitchen and downed a couple more drinks. This time I could taste the alcohol as it burned a path down my throat. Shawna looked to be even more affected by the drinks and I had to stop her from grabbing another one, instead leading her back out to the dance floor.

A couple of guys positioned themselves near us and took control of our movements. Shawna turned to face her partner, draping her arms around his neck without a care in the world. I leaned my head back to see my partner. His face was unfamiliar, and he stared down at me with a sexy grin. I figured one dance wouldn't hurt. We moved in sync and I let the music and alcohol wash over me, dulling my senses and letting me enjoy the moment.

The warm body behind me disappeared abruptly and I stumbled back having lost my support. I spun around to scold the stranger who had been dancing with me and came face to face with angry hazel-brown eyes. I threw my head back and sighed in annoyance before bringing my gaze back down to glare at Liam.

He leaned forward and hot breath tickled my ear as he whispered, "I thought I told you not to come here."

I stepped back and put my hands on my hips. "Like I said before, you cannot tell me what to do. I go where I please." I looked around to see where Shawna had gone but she was still dancing, however now there were two guys vying for her attention.

"Go home, Phi," Liam growled.

"Or what?" I tilted my chin up at him, feeling like a five-year-old but I didn't care.

His eyes narrowed and a small smile pulled at his lips. "Are you challenging me?"

My eyes widened, and I took a step back. Liam loved challenges and made it his mission to conquer every single one. He was dangerous and ruthless and would do anything to win. I did not want to challenge him. I caught myself before I took another step, knowing he would love the chase if I ran. Instead I stood my ground and pulled the nearest guy I saw to me and started dancing with him. The guy was only shocked for a second before accepting it and moving to the rhythm with me. Liam's jaw tightened and he stared me down for another second before walking away with clenched fists. I smiled in triumph and pushed him from my mind.

A few songs later, I was drenched in sweat and my hair stuck to my neck. I had no idea where Shawna went and the guy in front of me was new. I wondered when that happened. My partner led me to the kitchen where we leaned against the counter and took gulps of refreshing water and caught our breaths.

"You're an amazing dancer," the boy next to me complimented.

I smiled and put my cup down. "You're not too bad yourself."

He grinned and reached out, running his hand down my arm. My skin tingled and my breath caught. I wasn't completely sober yet, but my mind was clear enough to know what was about to happen. Was I going to let this stranger kiss me?

Glancing passed his shoulder I saw russet brown hair and green eyes. Kaden was on his way over to me. I quickly grabbed the stranger in front of me by his hand

and led him away from the kitchen to one of the halls that were not as crowded. I didn't want Kaden to yank this guy away like Liam did to the first one. When I figured we were safe, I released his hand and leaned against the wall. Misunderstanding my actions, the guy leaned forward and cupped the back of my neck, bringing my head closer to him. He leaned down and pressed his lips against mine. At first, I stood frozen, sandwiched between him and the wall but once I got my mind to understand what was happening, I brought my hands up between us and pushed him away.

He frowned. "What's wrong, I thought that's what you wanted."

My words stuck in my throat and I bit my lip instead. I didn't know what I wanted but I was pretty sure he wasn't it. The guy strode forward and kissed me again, trapping me with his arms, making it hard to break our contact this time. I shook my head to dislodge his mouth from mine, but he only laughed. My heart started racing with panic as I pushed against him, but he wouldn't move. Tears stung my eyes and I kicked my leg out at his shin which only made him crowd closer. I tried to bring up my hands again, but his body blocked them. I tried stepping on his feet and moving my head to the side again, but he had a firm grip on my neck and seemed unfazed by my stomping.

"Shh, it's ok, no need to fight it. I know this is what you want."

I felt sick and I was suddenly wishing I hadn't left the crowded room. Fear burned a path inside my chest and a sense of despair and loss filled me from head to toe causing a new kind of tears to spring forth. In addition to those feelings, anger caused the burning in my chest to spread and filled me until my lips seemed to burn too.

The guy gasped against my lips and suddenly fell back, freeing me. I collapsed and closed my eyes, feeling vulnerable and tired. I still felt that sense of loss and despair, but the burning anger was gone. I breathed in and out multiple times until I got my racing pulse under control. When I felt a little better, I opened my eyes. The sight of the boy that forced his kisses on me lying on the ground with black bubbles on his skin made me scramble back and scream. He looked like he was dead, but I couldn't be sure.

Three men appeared hulking over me and blocked the light. I screamed again hoping someone would hear me over the music. One of the shadowed men stepped forward and bent down so I could see them.

Relief washed through me at the sight of Liam. The other two stepped forward and I could finally see that they were Kaden and Trevor. Liam looked from me to the diseased looking corpse on the floor.

"It looks like you were right," Kaden said resignedly.

My eyes snapped up to Kaden, wondering what he meant by that.

"I was hoping I wasn't," Liam replied never taking his eyes from my face.

I was gathering the courage to ask what happened and demand answers but a crash from behind them halted my words. Liam sprang forward and scooped me up. I tried to look behind him to find out what had him spooked but he tucked my head against his chest making it impossible to see anything. I struggled against his hold, hating the helpless feeling coursing through my mind and body. I was just trapped against my will, I didn't feel like repeating it.

Liam finally stopped and glared down at me. "Stay in here and don't come out."

"Where-" I didn't get a chance to finish my question as I was dumped on the floor. Liam shut the door to whatever room I had been dumped in and I heard a click as the lock engaged. I scrambled up and banged on the door. "Let me out! You can't just lock me in here! That's illegal!" I wasn't sure if it was actually illegal, but I figured it could be considered kidnapping.

I put my ear to the door to try and hear what was going on but was met with only silence. Not even the music from the party penetrated the room. I decided waiting was my only option, so I looked around the room I had been put in. It was dark but I could just make out a broom and a toolbox, as well as some coats on hangers. Once I realized where I was, I gasped in outrage.

"No. You. Did. *Not*. Just lock me in a closet," I spoke out loud, though I knew Liam could not hear me.

I kicked the door and slumped against it. The image of the stranger's skin came to mind and I nearly gagged at the memory of those black boils. It looked like some kind of disease but how did he come down with it so fast? Was it infectious? I touched my lips in horror. Eww, was I going to suddenly break out in black bubbles and collapse? I stood up, frantic to get out and see a doctor. I banged against the door again shouting for someone to let me out.

The door opened as I was about to break through with my shoulder, causing me to lose my balance and fall forward. Trevor caught me and helped me get my balance before stepping away to give me space. I stared at him with wide eyes and looked around for the others.

"What hap-" A foul smelling cloth was placed over my mouth and nose from behind. I stared in fright at Trevor who stood by with a guilty look on his face. I struggled to remove the cloth but the longer it was there, the more the fight left me. The last thing I heard was Liam telling me to sleep then darkness took over.

"Phi, it's almost noon. Are you going to wake up anytime soon?"

The voice sounded familiar and I struggled to find consciousness so I could open my eyes and answer the concerned voice. A hand shook my shoulder helping to wake me up. I blinked open my eyes, wincing at the light from the window. Shawna's face appeared in my line of sight and relief washed over her face.

"Finally! I was worried you would sleep the whole day away." She helped me sit up and gave me some water.

"What happened?" An image of a dead body came to mind. I gasped and gripped Shawna's shoulders. "Is everyone okay?"

Shawna gave me a weird look before chuckling. "Um, as far as I know everyone is okay. Kaden and two other guys approached me at the party with you passed out in one of their arms. They said you had a bit too much to drink and were starting to cause a commotion. We brought you home and you have been sleeping ever since."

"Drank too much?" I looked at my blanket with furrowed brows.

Had all that other stuff been a dream then? My head hurt when I tried to recall the memories clearly. I was almost sure that I had seen a dead body and had been drugged. I drank some more water and figured I could ask the guys about it later. And by ask, I mean twist their ears and demand answers. I reached for my phone and pulled up my contacts but stopped when I realized I didn't have their numbers. I had deleted their numbers a year ago when I burned their motorcycles and never put them back in when I got a new phone. I sighed, resigned to having to wait until class on Monday before I could ask them anything.

"Hungry?"

The question surprised me, and I remembered Shawna saying that it was almost noon. My stomach grumbled in response. Shawna laughed and threw some clothes at me.

"Get dressed and we will go eat."

I did as she ordered, leaving the room to do my business in the communal bathroom. Looking in the mirror I gasped at the white streak in my hair. It was still an inch wide but now a second streak laid next to it. I groaned and tugged at the second streak. How was I going to explain that? I knew trying to get rid of it would be pointless, so I quickly finished my business and rushed back to my room.

When I came back, Shawna held her purse and a look of determination. If she noticed the new streak of white in my hair, she didn't show it. Instead she turned me around and marched me out of the room and down the hall. I was still kind of out of it, so I let her lead me to food not caring what kind it ended up being. We ended up in another student union on North campus with a little food court. My body immediately went to the Jamba Juice. Smoothies were life and I needed one. Shawna broke away to go get herself Einstein's bagels and coffee, leaving me alone to traverse the crowd in my half-asleep state. I made it to the line, got my smoothie, and headed toward Shawna who still waited on her food.

Halfway there, someone bumped into me roughly, causing my smoothie to tip over and fall to the floor, splattering delicious strawberry banana bliss all over the place. Students around the blast zone jumped away when some of it got on their clothes and gave me angry glares. I stared in shock at the smoothie on the ground then looked up to see who had done such evil. A girl with long blonde hair and blue eyes gave me a smirk and stared at me with hatred burning in her eyes. She wore what looked to be a letterman's jacket but instead of a letter there was a symbol of a cross with a sword overlapping it.

"Better watch where you're going next time. If I see you again you will regret it." The girl sauntered away never apologizing or looking back.

I stared at her retreating back with an open mouth, shocked that someone I didn't even know could hate me so much. Shawna came up to me a moment later, staring down at the mess on the floor.

"What happened here?" she asked, taking a sip of her coffee.

I swiveled my head to look at her, unsure how to explain what just happened. "Um, someone bumped into me."

Sudden anger washed through me and I snorted. If she ever saw me, *I* would regret it? If she ever saw me again, she better have back up. No one messed with my smoothie or threatened me. She was lucky I was too shocked to react that time.

Chapter 4

Monday rolled around and I was suddenly anxious to get to Math class. I sat in the same seat near the door that I had claimed last week and waited for the familiar dark hair and blue eyes of Trevor. The professor walked in a few minutes later but the seat next to me remained empty. I started tapping my foot against the floor impatiently. I had never known Trevor to miss a class. Another few minutes went by and the class officially started but Trevor never appeared. Had he finally realized he didn't need that class?

The basic Math class was stuff I had already gone over in high school, so it barely needed my attention. I took notes but my focus was on the door, though the more time that went by the more I realized he was not going to show up. By the end of class, I had resigned myself to having to ask Liam about Friday night, rather than Trevor. Once class ended, I quickly exited the Math building and raced over to the Language Arts building. I was fifteen minutes early and figured I would be able to talk to him a bit before class started. I grabbed a rolling desk-chair and sat near the back like usual and waited for Liam. The professor came in a few minutes later and started setting up his presentation. By that point I was spinning around in my seat as if I didn't have a care in the world but really, I was a mess on the inside. Were the guys ok? Had something happened to them? I stopped spinning and my heart began to race as a thought occurred to me. What if they contracted the same disease as that guy at the party? I was still not a hundred percent sure that was a real memory, but if it was then maybe they were already dead.

A knot formed in my throat at the idea. They weren't exactly my favorite people at the moment but that didn't mean I wished them dead. Just as I was about to have a mild panic attack, Liam walked through the door. The class immediately quieted as they watched him walk through the class. I expected him to sit next to me as he had done all last week, but he chose a seat on the opposite side of class near a group of girls. He never once turned his head to look at me despite my not-so-obvious attempts to get his attention. The girls giggled and leaned forward to touch his arm as they talked to him.

The professor called the start to class but I couldn't focus. I continued staring at the back of Liam's head urging him to turn and acknowledge me. I didn't understand what his problem was with me today. All last week they made it their mission to bug me and stalk me but now that I finally wanted to talk, they were nowhere near me.

At the end of class, Liam was the first one out. I struggled to push through everyone to reach him but when I finally got outside, he was nowhere to be seen. I sighed in frustration and decided I would just let it go for now. If something truly bad happened, I'm sure I would have heard about it through the rumor mill or on the news. Shawna surely would have heard something by now. I hopped on my bike and rode off to the Engineering building. The rest of the day went by smoothly and by smoothly, I mean the guys never appeared.

I was given a new project in one of my last Engineering classes and I decided to start working on it rather than worrying about Friday night's events. There was no point in worrying about something that probably didn't happen. I really did not want to go back to my room to study, knowing Shawna would want to go out somewhere which would put off our work. I would rather go somewhere quiet where I could be alone. The library came to mind and I smiled. I sent Shawna a quick text letting her know I would be back later and headed to the library.

I hadn't had the chance to go inside yet but when I did, it reminded me of the TARDIS from Doctor Who. The building made it look smaller, but the inside was enormous with four floors of countless twisting halls and hundreds of sections. I wondered how far back it went. I went to each floor and followed the stacks all the way back until I reached the other side. I enjoyed exploring, especially since there were not many people there.

On the third floor, I found the most confusing layout of the whole library. Instead of being set up in a grid system like the first two floors, the rows twisted and broke off to form new ones. After following some to try and find the end, I got lost. I stopped after passing the same study room for the third time. I checked my phone to look at a map of the library, but my phone didn't have any service which meant I could not use the internet. I guess I would study there until I had to leave, then I would worry about directions.

I found a nearby table and laid out my books and materials to start working on my project. It was silent in that part of the library. I felt relaxed and peaceful for the first time since I started my studies at Penn State. There was no one around to bother me, no one to bring up old memories, and no weird dreams to haunt me.

I was so absorbed in what I was doing that I nearly fell back in my chair when I heard a clanging noise from down the hall. I steadied my chair and held my hand to my chest, feeling my racing heartbeat calm. I waited for the person who made the noise to appear, but another clanging sound boomed down the hall. The noise got closer and my heartbeat picked up again. I stood up to face whatever was coming, suddenly feeling nervous and terrified since I was alone. I checked my phone again, hoping to be able to call Shawna but I still didn't have any service. The clanging sound occurred again but this time a curse followed it. I frowned at the voice, wondering who could be making that loud noise.

A metal library cart squeaked its way passed a shelf of books followed by an old lady. The cart crashed into a bookcase and the lady cursed again. I sighed in relief now that I finally knew what had been causing all the clanging.

The library lady noticed me and gave me an embarrassed smile. "I'm sorry dear, did I disturb you?"

Disturb was an understatement. She nearly gave me a heart attack, but I shook my head anyway. "The wheel giving you trouble?" I asked pointing to the wobbly front wheel that caused the cart to crash.

The woman put her hand on her head in exasperation. "You have no idea."

I walked over to the cart and knelt to take a look. After studying it a moment to find the problem I realized it was a loose bolt. I always kept a set of tools in my bag, so it shouldn't be too hard to fix. I quickly got up and rummaged through my backpack, finding my tools and bringing them back to the cart.

"Oh, honey you don't need-" the woman began to protest.

I cut her off with a wave of my tool in hand. "It will only be a minute." I straightened the wheel and tightened it up then stood when I felt confident it was fixed. "Try it out." I stood back to give her and the cart room to move.

She hesitantly pushed the cart a few feet. She turned to me with a wide grin. "Thank you dear! Now I don't have to struggle so much with this old thing."

"Any time." I waved goodbye as she took the cart and proceeded down the rows to do her library business.

Looking at my phone, I realized it was getting late. I walked back over to the study table and packed up my books. I tucked my tools in the side pocket of my backpack then shouldered the bag but paused before leaving. I still did not know how to get out of there.

Racing to the last place I saw the librarian I called out to her. "Hello, excuse me, I don't know where the exit is!"

I waited for an answer but was met with silence. Sighing I turned around and headed down the row the librarian had first come through. I would eventually run into a wall or someone then I could then find my way out. Just before I left the study area a noise stopped me.

A clanging sound against wood filled me with hope. I thought I had fixed the cart but at least now I could follow the noise and ask the librarian for directions.

I moved toward the noise and managed to get close to the last place it sounded from when a voice called out making me freeze. "Ophelia Bronson?"

Who knew my real name? I guess it could be someone from high school, but I didn't recognize the voice. At this point I didn't care. Anyone who could get me out of there would be fine.

"It's Phi actually, but yeah. Hello?" I called out.

A boy about my age stepped out from the stacks and smiled at me. I had no idea who he was but somehow, he knew my name. He had short blonde hair and blue eyes, but his jacket is what caught my attention. I had seen it before. More specifically, I had seen that sword overlapping a cross crest before. I was instantly on guard. I figured not everyone with that crest were mean but my only experience with it was bad.

My poor smoothie.

"I have been looking all over for you," the strange boy said in a bright cheery voice.

I narrowed my eyes at him, suspicious of his motives. Had that girl told him about our encounter and now he wanted to mess with me too? Maybe he was there to apologize for his companion's actions.

"You have? Why? And how do you know my name?" That gave me the biggest warning bells. I hadn't even told the blonde girl my name.

His cheery smile morphed into a scowl and he brandished a long metal sword from behind his back. I shouted in astonishment and nearly tripped over my feet as I tried to backpedal away from him. He advanced on me and raised the sword over his head. Complete determination and bloodlust shone in his eyes. I screamed and ran in the opposite direction.

How did he get a sword into a library without anyone noticing? More importantly, why was he trying to kill me with it?

I zigzagged my way down rows of bookshelves, doing my best to lose the maniac and find an exit. However, no matter how fast I ran he was always right behind me. A thunk near my head made me flinch. Looking up I saw a dagger stuck into the wooden bookshelf above me. I screamed again and ran down another row, not wanting a knife to impale me next.

I reached a wall but there was no door in sight. I would eventually find a way out if I followed the wall though, so I quickly made my way to the left, keeping the wall in sight. I glanced behind me to gauge the distance of the crazy boy. I couldn't see him anymore and took a deep breath in relief. I was hoping he gave up on chasing me, especially since someone must have heard me scream. Hopefully that old librarian I helped earlier.

I ran into a hard chest and stumbled back. I screamed again and swatted at the person I ran into, trying to defend myself. I would not go down without a fight even though I was completely outmatched. I felt bad for my parents in that moment. They would be even more crushed if their last child died. Hands wrapped around my flailing arms and forced them to my sides. My screams turned into sobbing as I pleaded with my attacker not to kill me.

"Shh, you're ok, tell me what happened. Why do you think I would kill you?"

At the soft tone, I looked up into familiar hazel-brown eyes. The eyes hardened when I didn't answer. "Who are you running from?" Liam ground out, concern evident in his voice.

I pointed behind me as my answer and leaned forward into Liam's chest. Liam wrapped me in his arms and let me cry. He smoothed my hair down which helped to calm me a bit, but my heart still pounded. He suddenly tensed and a deep rumbling sounded from his chest. I lifted my head and glanced at him curiously. His focus was on something behind me and I quickly spun, knowing I would see the scary sword wielder.

The boy stood there with his sword by his side as he glared at the two of us. "I should have known one of you would show up."

"You better turn now and leave if you know what's best for you," Liam practically growled.

My eyes widened at their exchange. Did Liam know this psychopath? Had I just run into the wrong arms? My heart told me I was safe with him though, so I relaxed a bit but kept my eye on the other boy.

"You four will destroy us all," the boy spat. He raised his sword and pointed it at us. "It is my duty to stop you."

He charged at us and I squeaked in terror. I tried running again but Liam held me tight, forcing me to stay put. I dug my nails into Liam's arm as I squeezed it, wanting us to move away from the sharp weapon. Fear washed over me, but it felt strange. Plenty of fear coursed through me already but this new feeling I was picking up on felt almost…unnatural. Unexpectedly, the boy stopped. His eyes widened in fear and his hands started to tremble. The sword dropped as the boy backed away slowly. I glanced around to see what had terrified him, but it was only Liam standing in the same spot, glaring at him. The boy turned and ran, leaving Liam and I standing alone with the fallen sword.

I waited to see if the guy would return but a minute passed with no more attacks. I stepped away from Liam, confused about what just happened. Why did the crazy guy change his mind? We were defenseless. He could have easily skewered us. I crossed my arms over my chest, partly because I was still scared and partly because I was angry.

"What the hell was that?" I decided to ask Liam, since he seemed to know that guy.

Liam closed his eyes and let out a long sigh. When he opened his eyes, he seemed disappointed that I was still there. Well, boohoo, someone just tried to kill me, and I needed answers. Liam studied me. The stare off was becoming awkward but I didn't want him to see how badly I was affected. On the inside, my body shook from the attack, but I kept a neutral expression on to hide it. I raised my eyebrow waiting for him to start talking.

"What happened is we were right," he finally said.

"You were right about what? You knew this would happen?" my voice was starting to border on the shrill side. If he admitted he knew I was going to be attacked tonight and didn't warn me then I would stomp over to that sword and stab him with it.

Liam bobbed his head side to side as if to say I was kind of correct. He walked forward and at first, I thought he was going to grab me again, but he moved past me and picked up the fallen sword. "It would be better to discuss this elsewhere. C'mon." He strode back the way he came leaving me no choice by to follow. I didn't want to be left there alone anyway. It would be a long time before I ever went to the library again.

Chapter 5

Liam led me away from the library, ignoring my every attempt to talk to him. His eyes stayed glued on our surroundings and eventually I stopped bugging him, knowing that I would get answers soon enough.

When he finally stopped, it was in front of a large two-story house on the edge of campus with steps leading up to the door. It looked familiar but I couldn't place where I had seen it before. Only when we were inside did I realize it was the house the party had been at on Friday. I was shocked the guys lived there and that they hosted the party where someone may or may not have died.

Liam led me into the kitchen, calling out, "I found her. Get down here," along the way.

Two sets of footsteps thundered down the stairs. Trevor and Kaden appeared with relieved grins on their faces. Liam threw the sword onto the table causing a loud clanging noise. I flinched at the sound, reminded of running through the stacks only a little while ago to get away from that sword.

"A Templar attacked her in the library," Liam said with anger tinging his tone.

"We figured that might happen," Trevor reminded him.

"Especially after Friday night," Kaden added.

I stayed quiet, hoping that if I did, they would spill some of the secrets they were hiding. However, I was bursting with questions. They practically admitted to something major happening at the party involving me and they somehow knew why a random college student attacked me. If they didn't get on with the explanations, I was going to pick up that sword and threaten them. Looking at the three guys though I realized I wouldn't get far with that tactic. Liam barely looked at a guy and sent him running. What hope did I have?

The three guys stared at me as if hearing my internal anxiety. I jumped when Trevor's hand landed on my shoulder and tried to calm my racing heart.

"You're probably wondering why you were attacked, right?" Kaden asked.

I narrowed my eyes at him and threw my hands in the air giving him my best *ya think?* look.

Trevor chuckled next to me and pulled out a chair. "I guess we better sit down. This is going to be a complicated discussion."

Liam gave out a long sigh and plopped into a chair. "I guess there's no way you will just go home and forget this ever happened?"

I shook my head and Liam put his head in his hands. Kaden held a chair out for me, and I slowly sank into it, knowing that once they explained whatever secret they were keeping, my life would be changed forever. Kaden sat in the last chair and we all stared at the sword laying in the middle.

Trevor blew air into his cheeks and let it out slowly. "Well, I guess we can start with this," he said gesturing to the sword.

I knew they were trying to figure out how much to tell me and in what order, but my patience was wearing thin. My body had finally stopped shaking from the traumatic event, but my mind was nearly going crazy from waiting for answers.

Kaden looked at Liam and Trevor with a raised eyebrow. When he realized they weren't going to start the conversation he leaned toward me and clasped my hands. I stared into his green eyes and felt a little calmer. Kaden had always been the kind, outgoing one so it was probably best for him to begin.

"The guy who attacked you with this," he gestured to the sword, "was part of a group called Order of the Templars."

I frowned trying to remember the stories of Templars in history. "I thought they were in Jerusalem or something."

"Yes, the main headquarters are but young Templars are sent on missions to the States and UK sometimes. Specifically, to places where we happen to be," Kaden explained.

"Why would they want to go where you three are?" I glanced at all their faces trying to pick up the answers from their expressions. "Aren't the Templars a religious thing?" I didn't mean for it to come out rude, but I had never seen them go to church or show any interest in religion.

"The main goal of the Templars is to protect holy sites and humanity from religious threats, so yes they are a religious thing," Trevor said fighting a smile at my words.

I nodded very slowly but what he said made no sense. If they stopped threats, then why were they at Penn State? What kind of threat could possibly be at a college? Images of the poor boy at the party collapsing with black boils on his skin came to mind. Was I the threat? I mentally shook my head at the idea. I would never hurt someone like that on purpose and I was no threat to humanity.

"That doesn't answer why they would be here." I looked at each one of them, but they avoided my eyes. "Why was I attacked tonight by a Templar?" My voice rose after each word, and the guys flinched.

Kaden leaned back and crossed his arms, refusing to be the one to say more. Trevor stood up and rifled through one of the cabinets bringing back a box of Ritz crackers. He started munching on the crackers making sure his mouth was full so he wouldn't have to talk, which meant Liam was the only one left. Liam stared at me with determination, but it was the sadness in his eyes that nearly made me get up and run. Whatever he was going to say I wasn't going to like it.

"We are the four Horsemen," he blurted.

Silence descended until all I heard was the crunching of crackers in Trevor's mouth. The only thing I knew about the four Horsemen was that they were the first part of the apocalypse. I stared at the boys around me. They were gorgeous and looked like traditional bad boys that rode motorcycles, but they didn't look like they could bring about an apocalypse. Maybe they were talking about a gang name or something.

"But there's only three of you," I pointed out. I decided I would assume they were talking about a gang rather than a religious prophecy.

The guys looked away but not before I saw anger and tragedy in their expressions.

"Owen was the fourth."

I didn't know who said it, but the words were like a soccer ball hitting me square in the chest. A lump formed in my throat and I tried to suck in air. I would not cry. I would not cry. I would *not* cry. "Owen?"

Liam looked back at me, reflecting the pain I would bet shown in my eyes. "We were the four Horsemen but the Templars," he cleared his throat before continuing, "the Templars got to him. Made it look like an accident."

I stood up, knocking my chair back loudly and walked backwards until my back hit the wall. "Accident?" I whispered.

"We thought that would be the end of it, but they showed up during graduation," Kaden added.

My head whipped to him. "They were at graduation?" I clenched my fists. They had to be messing with me, but it was cruel to use my dead twin brother as part of their prank. I glanced at the sword, wondering if I could get to it fast enough.

The three guys stood up as well and stepped closer to me until they were in a half circle, blocking my exit.

"We dealt with them, but that was when we realized that maybe you were in danger, even though…" Kaden trailed off.

I glared at him. "Even though they already killed my brother?"

They nodded and that was the last straw. I crumpled and would have hit the floor if it wasn't for Liam's strong arms catching me. He held me up and let me sob into his shirt as all the emotions I had pushed back over the year came flooding out.

The doctor said Owen was in a motorcycle accident. After hearing that I went to the guys' houses and burned their motorcycles down not wanting anyone else to die because of those death machines. I also burned them partly because I blamed Owen's three best friends for his death. They were the ones to get him into motorcycles and living on the dangerous side. Was there more to the story? Had it truly been murder rather than an accident?

I don't know how long I cried but the guys never left my side. Eventually I reigned in my emotions and stepped back, drying my face with the back of my hands. I sniffled a few times until Kaden handed me a tissue. I turned away and blew my nose then walked slowly to the other side of the kitchen to throw it away. My hand found the beads of my bracelet and I stood on shaking legs, fiddling with them. Seeking some comfort and familiarity. I was stalling but I couldn't escape the truth forever.

I turned to them with clenched fists. "What kind of messed up gang life are you in and why am I being dragged into it?" I was angry all over again. Angry at them for dragging my brother into their gang and angry that they were now trying to put me in danger alongside them. I knew seeing them at orientation and in my classes spelled out trouble.

Trevor shook his head and stepped towards me, but I backed up, not wanting them to be close to me. Hurt flashed over his face before he masked it with a neutral expression. "We are not part of a gang. We are the real four Horsemen."

I stood there a moment with my mouth agape then started laughing. The real Horsemen? As in the harbingers of the apocalypse? The ones who are destined to spread war and disease? Ok, maybe they were not involved with gang stuff, but I was starting to think they were involved with drugs.

Liam glowered at me and the other two held solemn expressions. My laughing died away when they didn't join, and I realized they truly believed they were the Horsemen. "Why do you think that?"

"We don't think that, we know it," Liam countered. "And it's a long story, all you need to know is that we are." He crossed his arms as if it was final and there would be no room for discussion.

Trevor rolled his eyes at Liam then pointed at me. "Yeah, and you are the fourth."

My jaw dropped again at their declaration. "What makes you believe that?"

"Well, first off your brother used to be one of the four," Kaden started.

My brother, a Horseman? Yeah right, I would have known. Right?

"He was Death," Trevor added.

My heart clenched at his words. Were they just saying that because he was dead? They must have read the thought on my face because they all stepped forward to explain the rest before I blew up in their faces.

"We think you are the fourth because you are his twin, you have the same white streaks in your hair, and um," Kaden looked uncomfortable, "you used your power on Friday."

My power? Did they mean the black bubbles that caused that college guy to die? "That was real?" I whispered.

My stomach turned and I felt I would be sick any moment. They must have seen the discomfort because they quickly placed me in a chair and handed me a glass of water. I fought to control my roiling stomach.

Kaden raised his hand. "I'm War."

I frowned at his announcement. Kaden seemed like the least war type person I have ever known. He hated conflict, not that it stopped him when he was forced to fight.

Trevor nodded as he reached into his Ritz box to grab another cracker. "I'm Famine."

Despite my queasiness, I nearly snickered at that idea because he ate all the time. It seemed like a contradiction.

I glanced at Liam who had been quiet for a while. "And if I am to believe all this, that makes you Conquest?" I mentally patted myself on the back for knowing the story.

He gave me a nod and met my eyes daring me to doubt him. His role I could believe. He loved challenges and always had to be the best. He was not considered the King of our high school for nothing. However, if they were the

Horsemen then why hadn't the apocalypse happened yet? They also mentioned a power. If mine caused death, I almost gagged at the idea, then what could they do? I had known them for years and not once had they expressed a power or hungering for death and destruction. I was almost too scared to ask, plus I didn't know if I could handle any more information right now.

My body felt weak and my mind was overloaded. I stood up preparing to leave. "I think I should go get some sleep."

"You are going to stay here tonight," Liam ordered.

I raised my eyebrows at his authority. "No, I'm going to go home. I have classes tomorrow." Ha! As if I could focus on class after all that.

Liam stood and walked up to me until he was only inches from my body. I knew he was expecting me to back away ultimately showing weakness, but I stood my ground. If he truly was Conquest, then he probably wasn't used to someone standing up to him. Well, he was about to figure out that I was not someone who could be conquered.

"It's not safe," he whisper-growled.

I could see Trevor and Kaden in my peripherals exchanging amused looks, but I kept my eyes focused on Liam. "You can't tell me what to do."

A slow smirk pulled at his lips. I've seen that look before. It's his I-accept-the-challenge smirk. I shook my head and sighed. I didn't want to deal with him anymore. I walked around him and made my way to the door.

"I can take care of myself," I threw over my shoulder.

My feet caught on something and I tripped, letting out a squeak of surprise as I fell to the floor. I looked up from the ground to see Liam grinning down at me. Did he just trip me?

"I can see that, High Phi," he said sarcastically.

Snickers sounded from behind him and I did my best to give the three of them my finest glare. I got up and dusted myself off before turning back to the door.

"Phi, wait," Kaden called out.

I paused but didn't turn around. "We are serious about it not being safe. We don't know if more Templars will try to attack you tonight," Trevor finished.

The thought of someone coming at me with a sword again filled me with terror. Worry slid its way into my mind when I thought about Shawna getting caught in the middle. I couldn't put her in danger. I turned slowly and slumped in defeat. "Fine, but only for tonight. I can't stay here forever."

"We'll see," Liam said quietly.

His face stayed blank when I looked at him sharply. I wasn't sure if he meant for me to hear that or not.

Kaden stepped forward and took my hand, guiding me away from the other two. "You can sleep in the guest room. I will take you."

I followed him up the stairs, exhaustion making my feet heavy. I didn't want to admit it, but I felt safer staying there rather than trekking home on my own to face whatever may be out there. I sent a quick text to Shawna to let her know where I was and that I wouldn't be home. She immediately sent a reply demanding details in the morning. I chuckled. I don't think being attacked and told I am the new Death is what she had in mind.

Kaden stopped in front of a door and held out an arm toward it. "Here you are. Let us know if you need anything."

Kaden started to walk away but I called out, stopping him. Curiosity and a bit of hope had been nagging me since they told me my brother was Death. "Um, if Owen was uh, Death, then does that mean he controlled it?"

Kaden's face screwed up showing me he was about to dash my hope though he hated to do it. "I know what you're thinking but no he couldn't bring back the dead and neither can you."

My shoulders slumped in disappointment. I believed their story of the Horsemen mainly because I was hoping Death meant we couldn't die but Owen was truly gone. What was the point of being Death if we could die? I was angry at the universe for making it that way. If it wasn't for the fact that I had witnessed my supposed powers at work, and I was attacked earlier by a Templar then I would have refused to believe them anymore.

Kaden leaned forward and gave me a hug. "I miss him too, Phi."

I pressed my lips together and squeezed my eyes shut to stop the tears building in them. When I knew I had my emotions under control, I spun around and opened the guest bedroom door. I darted inside and quickly closed the door before he could say anything else. I heard him go down the stairs and I relaxed a bit. Maybe if I went to sleep then all the crazy stuff would go away.

Chapter 6

Nightmares assaulted my mind all night long. Nightmares about crashing motorcycles and an army of college students with swords hunting me. The worst one was about a grim reaper on a pale horse holding a scythe as it chased me. I tried to run from it but could never get away. When the reaper caught me, it held me in its grip and folded back its hood to show my brother's face with his floppy black hair and white streaks in it same as mine. He looked skeletal, bone peeking through his gaunt skin, eyes sunken in. It made me scream until I woke up. That nightmare occurred three times in the night. Each time, one of the guys would barge through the bedroom door to see if I was alright. I continued to send them away promising I was fine, but it made sleep difficult.

My alarm went off, but I was already awake. I didn't want to get up and go to classes as if everything was normal, but I also didn't want to fall behind in my second week of school. Groaning, I rolled over until I had no choice but to get up or fall to the floor. I trudged out of the room to the bathroom down the hall, thankful none of the guys were around to see my disheveled state. Also, I wasn't sure I could handle seeing supernatural Horsemen yet.

I stared at myself in the mirror, trying to see if anything was different. I scowled at my reflection. My hair was a mess and my clothes were rumpled but nothing else stood out. I pulled at the skin below my eyes trying to make my eyes look skeletal like Owen's in my dream. It only made me look crazy, so I dropped my hands. How could I be a supernatural entity? It was impossible.

I lifted one of the white streaks in my hair and stared at it. My brother had white streaks in his hair. The only difference between mine and his was that mine appeared a year ago. Owen had his since birth. Did that mean he was born to be Death? I shivered at the thought.

A knock on the bathroom door startled me.

"I have some clothes for you," Trevor called through the door.

I frowned. How did they get clothes for me? Had they stopped by my dorm room or bought some new ones? I opened the door a crack to peer through.

Trevor stood there in pajama bottoms, a black t-shirt, and rumpled hair that did nothing to retract from his gorgeous looks. A black tattoo of old-fashioned scales peeked from under his left shirt sleeve. He held a bag and extended it to me when he saw me through the crack in the door. I quickly snaked out an arm, grabbed the bag, and pulled it into the bathroom without having to reveal my whole body.

"Thanks." I shut the door without waiting for a response.

I picked through the garments in the bag, curious about what they brought me. Surprisingly, I saw a familiar black t-shirt, dark pants, underwear and matching bra. I found my toothbrush, hairbrush, and deodorant in the side pockets. They must have stopped by my dorm at some point. I wondered how they got inside. Shawna had explained to me that our IDs were programmed to the dorm we stayed in to give us access. If speaker boy let them in without a programmed ID, I was going to hunt him down and smack him. I pictured the guys combing through my drawers and heat filled my cheeks. I was overreacting. Shawna was probably the one who gathered the items and put them into a bag.

I took my time getting ready even though I knew I would be late to class if I hung out there any longer. When I emerged from the bathroom three sets of eyes landed on me. I covered my shock with a scowl. "That's creepy. You could have waited downstairs."

Liam smirked at me. "Took you long enough, we thought you might have drowned in there."

I shook my head and pushed passed them to go to class. Liam chuckled and three sets of footsteps followed behind me.

At the front door I turned to stare at them. They were only a couple feet away but stopped when I turned. I was scared to go out there where Templars might attack but I didn't want to tell them my fear. My hesitancy spoke loud enough though.

Trevor stepped forward and draped his arm over my shoulders, guiding me to the door and outside. "Don't worry, one of us will be with you at all times."

"I hope not at *all* times," I said thinking about them trying to follow me into the bathroom.

His face reddened and I fought down a smile at his embarrassment. I may have sounded like I was joking but I really did not want to be followed everywhere. I knew Trevor was trying to be helpful but having them around me all the time did not bode well for my life. Yes, I was scared, but no I did not need a babysitter.

I shrugged off his arm. "You guys don't need to follow me around everywhere. You must have better things to do."

They all stared at me unblinking. I couldn't read anything from their expressions but none of them were backing down, so I assumed I was stuck with them for now. I sighed and started walking away then threw over my shoulder, "Fine, but you guys have to tell me everything about all this Horsemen stuff then."

Liam chuckled as he passed me, his hands in his pockets and backpack slung over one shoulder. "Not a chance." He stopped any discussion on the topic by walking ahead to go to class.

Kaden shrugged apologetically but followed Liam. I glared at their backs then headed to my first class, assuming Trevor would be right behind me since he shared Math with me. Thankfully, their house was not too far away from campus, so I didn't have to walk that much. I would have to stop by the library sometime today to retrieve my bike, but for now I was fine.

Trevor eventually caught up and we walked to class side by side. Questions burned in the back of my throat, wanting to be released but I held back. I wasn't sure if I was allowed to talk about any of it out in the open, so I kept glancing around trying to pick up any strange behavior from students. Thankfully, I got to class without anyone attacking me and ten minutes to spare. We claimed our usual seats by the door where I eyed everyone who came in suspiciously. When no one else wandered in, I glanced at Trevor, trying to see anything different that may point out his supernatural identity. He claimed he was Famine. What did that entail? What were his powers?

"What's on your mind, Phi?"

His voice startled me, and I snapped my head around to stare at the board rather than him. "Nothing."

"I can tell you're curious. You can ask me anything," Trevor said low enough so only I could hear him.

I looked around to see if anyone was listening, but all the students seemed to be in their own conversations. I was glad Trevor did not hold the same rule that Liam tried putting in place about not letting me learn about them. Us. Whatever.

I leaned closer to Trevor anyway and asked, "What are your, um, powers?"

I felt stupid asking someone that in real life. Powers? Really? But I couldn't deny what happened to that boy at the party. I was eighty, no, ninety percent sure I did that. I was both intrigued and frightened by this new world. That probably made me a little evil. A scary thought came to mind. Were we born evil?

"Well, all of our, um, powers," he gave me an amused look at the word powers, "deal with emotions and human needs." He stared at me for a long moment, but I didn't understand what he was saying.

His icy, blue eyes unnerved me. Trevor reached out and touched the top of my hand lightly with his fingers. My skin tingled and a sharp pang hit me hard in the stomach. I should have eaten breakfast before I rushed out of the house. Trevor's fingers glided along my hand to my wrist and up my arm sending chills racing through my whole body. My stomach clenched and I gasped at how hungry I was. I wanted Trevor to finish what he was saying about playing on emotions, but I couldn't focus anymore. All I could think about was how empty my stomach was and how desperate I was becoming for food.

"Do you-" without thinking I gripped his shirt and yanked him near me, "do you have any food with you?" I let go of his shirt as another pang of hunger swept through me, followed by despair. I put my hands over my stomach trying to contain the overwhelming feeling. What was I thinking? Of course, he didn't have any food. No one had food. I was going to die right there in the classroom and fulfill the Templars' wish. Tears sprang to my eyes at the hopelessness I felt. No one could help me and there was no point in fighting for life anymore.

Suddenly the feeling of hunger and despair vanished as if it was never there to begin with. Realization hit me. I sucked in a sharp breath and stared wide eyed at Trevor. "You did that?"

He nodded, as he sat back and crossed his arms. His brown leather jacket strained against his arms, but he didn't seem to mind. I didn't think anyone in there minded either if the admiring looks from the girls behind us was any indication.

"How did you do that?" I asked in wonder. I hated the feelings he caused but I was fascinated that he had the ability to do it.

"We all influence emotions and needs in some way." The professor walked in at that moment cutting off any response I would have made. He called the beginning to class but before we got too far, Trevor leaned over and whispered, "We will teach you."

I knew Liam would refuse but it was nice that I could count on Trevor and possibly Kaden. I couldn't focus on Math after that. I was too busy imagining what my powers were. I shuddered at the thought of causing someone to die of black boils again, but I had to be able to do something else. According to Trevor, each of us effected needs or emotions. Trevor caused hunger and despair. Kaden was War so maybe he caused anger or hatred. Liam was Conquest but I couldn't figure out what emotion he would influence. The guy in the library looked afraid after Liam stared at him so maybe fear was his power. I would have to ask them later how I caused death instead of an emotion so I could avoid it in the future. Had Owen gone through a trial and error phase? Shame flooded my body and made me hate myself. How could I call killing someone a trial and error? That was horrible.

Trevor nudged my arm an hour later, bringing me out of my thoughts. I glanced down at my notebook and realized I had only taken one note. I sighed. I couldn't keep that up if I wanted to pass. Students shuffled by our seats chatting or rushing to get to their next class. I scrambled up and grabbed my bag giving Trevor a thankful nod before walking to my English class. Trevor followed me most of the way to make sure I was safe then headed off to whatever class he had next.

I decided I would sit next to Liam instead of avoiding him. I had more questions that needed to be answered and he was just the guy to have them. I walked into the classroom to find I was the first of few to arrive which meant I had to wait anxiously for Liam. I snagged a rolling desk chair near the back and eyed the door. Every time someone walked through my heart raced in anticipation only to be slowed when a stranger came through instead. I tapped my foot impatiently and eventually the professor walked in. I would only have a couple of minutes to talk before class started.

Where was Liam?

"Alright everyone, let's-" the professor began but cut off when the door opened again.

Liam sauntered through, his backpack slung over one shoulder, his hand in his pocket. His eyes found mine and narrowed. Without a glance at the teacher and not caring he was late he walked to the back of the room and sat in one of the rolling desk-chairs.

"Now that everyone is here," the professor said with a pointed look at Liam, "Let's begin." The teacher turned toward the board and began his lesson.

My senses were hyperaware of Liam though, so I heard nothing the professor taught. Out of the corner of my eye I watched Liam roll his desk closer to mine. Girls around the room kept glancing at him, trying to get his attention but he managed to ignore them. Surprisingly.

I wanted to talk to him about everything, but I also did not want to draw attention to us by interrupting the lecture, even if we were whispering. A piece of paper landed on my desk. I stared at it for a long moment before looking up at Liam, who stared at me then the paper with a pointed look. I opened the piece of paper, feeling like an elementary student reading notes behind the teacher's back.

How'd you sleep?

I tensed. He knew exactly how I slept since each of them took turns checking on me every time I woke up from a nightmare. I looked up frowning, thinking he was messing with me. For once, he was not smirking or goading me. Instead, his eyes shone with concern and his fingers twitched as if he wanted to reach out and touch me. I let down my guard a bit and wrote a short reply.

Fine. So, Trevor tells me your powers effect emotions.

No sense in beating around the bush. I tossed the note to him but kept my eyes on the teacher to make sure he didn't see. A second later a snort drew my attention. I turned to see Liam smirking at the paper and writing a response. What was so funny?

First off, we don't call them powers, they are talents. And

secondly...

Talents. Trevor hadn't mentioned that, but it was probably better to say the word talents than powers if someone happened to overhear. I glanced up wondering what he meant by secondly and saw him trying to fight a smile. Oh, it was going to be like that, huh?

Secondly...

Secondly, you should pay attention to the lecture.

I narrowed my eyes at the note then him. He avoided my look, but I knew he saw it from the way a smile tugged at his lips. I scribbled a reply, demanding he tell me more about the four Horsemen then threw it at his desk, feeling a bit exasperated. Liam opened it to read what I wrote then tucked it into his jeans pocket without replying.

I felt like grumbling, but I held back as that would draw attention to myself. I didn't know why I thought Liam would talk to me about it all. He liked toying with me, I could tell. Well, joke's on him because I knew two other guys who would answer all my questions. I bit my lip as I stared at the clock waiting for class to end. Even though none of the guys technically had anymore classes with me today, I knew Kaden or Trevor would be in my Engineering class anyway. Only, I would have to find a way to talk to them without drawing Shawna's attention.

I bit my lip and tapped my pen against my notebook, waiting for the teacher to call the end to class. A note landed on my desk and I stared at it with excitement. I guess Liam decided to tell me something after all.

You're cute when you bite your lip.

I turned and scowled at Liam, making sure he saw me crumple up the paper before I tossed it back at him. I was annoyed with his games and his playboy attitude. I was not just going to fall over myself after one compliment and forget my quest for answers. Thankfully, students began to stand and gather their stuff, signaling the end of class. I quickly stood and shoved my book into my bag before making a quick exit from class. I only had twenty minutes to get to Engineering Design and I wanted free time to talk before it began.

I saw Liam stalking me a few feet behind but gave him a smug grin when a gaggle of girls blocked his path, trying to get his attention. I was free for a little bit and he would not be able to stop me from finding out more.

As I suspected, Kaden ended up suddenly enrolling in Engineering Design despite it not having anything to do with his major in communications. I caught him leaning against a wall outside the class, talking to a few girls. Once he caught my eye, he excused himself and came over to me. I glanced inside and saw Shawna already sitting at the front, but I wanted to ask Kaden a few things first.

"Hey," Kaden greeted and flashed his perfect smile. I was sure that was how he got those girls to stay by his side before I showed up. That and his charm he seemed to exude constantly.

I pulled him away from the classroom where students were streaming in, not wanting anyone to overhear. "So,

Liam was no help, but Trevor told me about your guys' powers, er, talents. You're War, right?" He nodded but frowned at the topic I was bringing up. "So, what kinds of emotions do you trigger? What could Owen do? Can I do the same things?" I hoped I wasn't bombarding him too much, but I was eager for answers.

He crossed his arms and thought about my questions. After a few moments he looked at me apologetically. "I don't think Liam wants us to be telling you anything."

I grunted in annoyance. "You are a big boy so pull up your big boy drawers and think for yourself."

Kaden stared at me in astonishment then burst into laughter causing a few people passing by to look toward us curiously. When he got it all out of his system he said laughingly, "Right you are."

I continued staring at him expectantly and his face sobered. "Man, I'm gonna be in trouble for giving you information but screw it. As War I can cause overwhelming anger and direct it toward whatever I choose. I can also use other people's natural anger to fuel my strength."

My eyebrows rose as I imagined what that would be like. If it was anything like Trevor's talents, then I would be happy to stay far from it. I was pleased though that I had guessed Kaden's talent correctly.

"Liam causes fear which helps him conquer just about anything, and Trevor can cause despair and hunger," Kaden continued, unaware of my thoughts. "Owen," pain tinged his voice, "he could cause sickness both emotionally and physically."

I nodded. It seemed like that was my talent as well. I was pleased to know my talent was controllable and that I didn't have to kill someone by using it. The only thing I had to do was practice and there was no way I was going to do that on innocent people.

"C'mon, let's go to class." Kaden turned toward the room and motioned for me to follow.

I guess he was done answering my questions for now but that was okay. I had much to think over and much to hide from my roommate who would surely want details of my overnight adventures.

Chapter 7

Shawna ogled the three men sitting across from us. She probably thought she was being discreet but there was no way they didn't notice her stare. Shawna had been excited that Kaden was in our Engineering Design class and spent the whole hour flirting with him. She had invited him and his friends to lunch with us and now we sat at one of the many tables in the dining area in awkward silence. Well, maybe it was only awkward for me. The guys didn't seem to mind being mentally stripped by my roommate's eyes, but it made me want to gag.

Liam smirked at me making me wonder if one of his talents was mind reading. I quickly dismissed that idea however, since Trevor had said our talents effected emotions and needs. And I did not *need* him to read my mind.

"So, what are your majors?" Shawna asked directing the question to all but trailing a finger over Kaden's hand on the table.

Kaden leaned forward and flashed a dazzling smile at my new friend. I was pretty sure she may have swooned.

Bleh!

"Communications," Kaden answered.

Shawna frowned momentarily before smoothing it over with a flirtatious smile. She was probably wondering what a Communications major was doing in an Engineering class.

"Economics," Trevor added, from the other side of the table. I wasn't surprised by his answer. He had always been fascinated with Economics and Math.

We turned our heads to Liam who was last to answer. His gaze settled on me and a slow smile pulled at his lips. "Where best to conquer the world than Business?"

I rolled my eyes and turned my attention to the table and food in front of me. I still felt his gaze upon me, but I refused to look. Kaden and Trevor had told him about my questions and the answers they gave. I knew he was trying to intimidate me by reminding me he was Conquest. Trying to make me see there was no point in going against his wishes since he always got his way. Well, he should know by now that I, Ophelia Bronson, bowed down to no one. I would learn about the whole four Horsemen thing whether he liked it or not. Why was he so worked up about a couple of questions anyway? He had to have known telling me who we were would only add fuel to the fire of curiosity.

Dark, slender fingers snapped in front of my face bringing me back to the conversation. I followed the fingers to their owner and found Shawna's smile trained on me. "I said how was last night?"

I glanced briefly at the guys, but they all had matching masks of indifference. They were too good at that. "Um, alright I guess, I ran into Liam at the library and decided to hang with them and catch up. Time passed and before I knew it, I was too tired to leave."

Shawna's eyes narrowed a bit. I would be suspicious too if I were in her shoes. Last time we talked about Liam, Kaden, and Trevor, I complained about them but now I was suddenly okay with them. She knew I was lying but I kept my face composed. After a moment of scrutiny, she sat back with a bright smile and let the topic drop.

For the rest of lunch, I let Shawna continue leading the conversation while we ate. Eventually, Shawna's phone beeped reminding her of her next class. "Oh man, I gotta go. Text me later," she told me then lowered her voice into a husky tone and wiggled her fingers at Kaden, "Bye, call me." Then she was gone, leaving the four of us alone.

I couldn't help but burst into laughter. Kaden stared at me with confusion while the other two hid smiles. "She is so into you." I grew serious and leaned in toward Kaden so he could hear me better. "Don't ever hurt her or you will be on the receiving end of some serious illness." At that moment my threat was an empty one because I didn't know how to cause sickness on demand yet, but he didn't need to know that.

Trevor and Liam's fight to contain their humor failed at my threat and they started laughing. Even Kaden chuckled which only made me grumpy. The least they could do was take my threat seriously.

We had an hour left until my next class and I did not really want to spend it sitting there in the cafeteria. "I'm gonna go get my bike."

I stood and headed for the door without waiting for a reply. I didn't turn back until I exited the building, but I wasn't surprised to find the three of them following me when I did. I stopped, waiting for them to reach me so I could talk to them. There was no point walking alone when I could be getting answers.

"So how did you guys find out you were Horsemen?" I asked, watching their expressions carefully.

The three of them stiffened. It was Liam who answered but his answer made me want to smack him. "None of your business." Then he walked ahead, leading us to the library.

I glared at his back but when he didn't look at me, I gave into my temptation and pinched him.

"Ow!" A very fierce, very tall Horseman turned on me and suddenly invaded my personal space. "What did you do that for?" Liam asked calmly, but fire burned in his hazel-brown eyes.

"I-" I glanced at the other two, but they didn't seem inclined to help me. Liam smirked at my hesitation which made me stand straighter and put my fists on my hips. "How can you say it's none of my business? I am part of this now and whether you like it or not, Liam Griffiths," I poked him in the chest eliciting a growl from him. "I will learn everything about it."

Sudden and sharp fear washed through me making me shake. My heart raced until I thought it would jump out of my chest. I did not know why I thought standing up to him would be a good idea. Why did I need to know about the Horsemen? It was all too dangerous for me. My heart pumped so frantically I thought it would burst from my chest. My legs started shaking and my finger trembled. If I didn't run away, I was afraid I might die. I started to turn to run to the library far, far away from that towering, terrifying man.

Something Kaden said earlier niggled in the back of my mind, trying to overcome the fear triggering my flight response.

Liam causes fear which helps him conquer just about anything.

I yanked my finger from his chest and the fear evaporated. I gaped at Liam as I held my finger as if I had been shocked. "Did you just try to use your talent to make me drop the subject?"

Liam looked annoyed that his plan had not worked. The nerve! I swept past him and marched away.

My bike was exactly where I left it by the library. I unlocked it, glad that it had not been stolen, and without looking back I hopped onto it and rode off toward my dorm. Shouts sounded behind me, but I ignored them. I needed some me time.

When I reached my dorm, I quickly locked my bike to the rack then rushed inside, pleased that only residents could enter with their ID. Even if the boys caught up to me, they would not be allowed inside. That is unless speaker boy let them in, in which case I would have some words. I waited five minutes anyway, sure that they would find some way to reach me. I sat at my desk staring at the door, but no one came. I decided to push them out of my thoughts and get some homework done before I fell behind. I took out my books, and for the next half hour focused only on my work.

A while later, the door handle jiggled causing my heart to race. How did they get into the Residence Hall? I closed my books, and stood, ready to take a stance and kick them out. A familiar pretty, tall woman with mocha skin and curly brown hair entered the room.

I breathed out a sigh and gave my roommate a bright smile. "Oh, it's just you." I sat back down in my desk chair and put my homework away.

Shawna frowned at my comment but smiled back. "Thanks, nice to be welcomed," she said sarcastically.

I chuckled, "No, I was just expecting someone else and was glad when it was you instead."

Shawna raised a thin eyebrow at me. "Trouble with the boys?"

I nodded but didn't elaborate. Shawna pulled some books out of her bag and threw them on her desk. The top one read *Religions of the World.* A thought struck me, and I leaned forward in anticipation. "Shawna you take a Religion Studies class, right?" I didn't wait for her answer, the book being an obvious indicator. "Do you perhaps have a Bible or any stories about apocalypses?"

Shawna chuckled, "Apocalypses? Why the sudden interest?" She pulled a Bible from her desk drawer and handed it over.

A quick Googling of the four Horsemen told me I would find the story in the book of Revelation. I could have just continued my research online, but I knew how stories changed and got twisted around for entertainment on the internet. I wanted to learn the story that the Templars based their whole mission on. Shawna studied me curiously, but I just turned away and read to myself.

Then I saw when the Lamb broke one of the seven seals, and I heard one of the four living creatures saying as with a voice of thunder, "Come." I looked, and behold, a white horse, and he who sat on it had a bow; and a crown was given to him, and he went out conquering and to conquer.

That was obviously about Conquest. No wonder Liam thought he was king of everything. It was written in the Bible that a crown was given to the first Horseman.

However, this couldn't be talking about Liam Griffiths. That would make him over 2000 years old. This was about the first appearance of the Horsemen.

When He broke the second seal, I heard the second living creature saying, "Come." And another, a red horse, went out; and to him who sat on it, it was granted to take peace from the earth, and that men would slay one another; and a great sword was given to him.

Kaden came to mind, but I couldn't picture him taking peace from the earth. However, he was born with the talent to cause anger and in many cases, anger is the opposite of peace and the beginnings of war. It was so strange to match the story with the real thing though.

When He broke the third seal, I heard the third living creature saying, "Come." I looked, and behold, a black horse; and he who sat on it had a pair of scales in his hand.

The rest of the verse spoke of wheat and barley being sold for something called a denarius, but my mind skipped over it. I understood it was trying to say the black horse rider was Famine, but I didn't understand the wording. It was interesting that the story spoke of Famine holding scales. I remembered seeing a tattoo of scales on Trevor's arm that morning. Did the rest of the guys have tattoos? Owen never spoke of having one but then again, he could have kept it hidden. Our mother would have flipped.

My heart raced as I read about the last Horseman. The one about me and Owen.

When the Lamb broke the fourth seal, I heard the voice of the fourth living creature saying, "Come." I looked, and behold, an ashen horse; and he who sat on it had the name Death; and Hades was following with him. Authority was given to them over a fourth of the earth, to kill with sword and with famine and with pestilence and by the wild beasts of the earth.

Kill. Pestilence. I guess that really was my destiny. I slammed the book shut, angry at the destiny it portrayed. It made us evil and the bringers of the end of the world. No wonder the Templars wanted to kill us. Why were the Horsemen even created? I opened the book, remembering something from each verse. It was a lamb that opened the seals and released the Horsemen. The lamb of God apparently. How is the end of the world our fault then? The Templars needed to rethink who they were hunting.

"Don't you have a class soon?" My roommate's voice dragged me out of my thoughts of lambs and Horsemen.

I bolted up out of my chair and grabbed my bag. "Shoot, right, thanks!" I shouted as I rushed from our room.

Thank goodness I got my bike back. I only had ten minutes to get to my last class of the day. I wondered who would be in class with me. War, Famine, or Conquest.

I got to my class just in time to watch the professor walk in behind me. Hey, if I got there first then I wasn't late. I took a seat in the back of class since those were the only ones left open and pulled out my notebook. Even if I was going to keep with the theme today of not doing notes, I could at least act like it.

Someone plopped into the seat beside me and leaned in. "Almost thought you weren't going to make it," Liam joked.

I glared at him then turned my attention to the professor who began his lesson. Liam sat back with his hands behind his head but did not say anymore. His silence allowed me to focus on my education, but I was still aware of his presence. I wanted to ask about what I read in the Bible about the apocalypse, but I had learned my lesson. I wouldn't get any answers from Liam so there was no point in pestering him about Horsemen stuff.

At the end of class, the students shuffled out, and I stood to join them. I turned to Liam but didn't know what to say so I waved awkwardly and headed out with my backpack slung over my shoulder. Liam caught up to me and grabbed my shoulder turning me to face him. I was about to slap his hand and scold him for forcing me to stop but the look on his face stopped me.

He studied me with a frown but not angrily, rather, curiously. "You're not going to stop, are you?" he finally spoke.

I huffed in annoyance. "Stop what?"

"You're going to hurt yourself if you try to learn more on your own. C'mon." With that he shoved his hands in his pockets and walked from the classroom.

I frowned at his back, confused by his words. I ran to catch up to him and found him next to my pale colored bike outside. He stared at it with a small smile but lost his amusement when he saw me looking.

"What did you mean earlier?"

He turned to face me fully and chuckled. "You're too stubborn so if we are going to do this then let's start by going for dinner."

I shook my head and held out my hand to stop him. "Whoa, whoa, if we are to do this? Do what?"

He looked exasperated and begrudgingly said, "If we are going to teach you about us."

My eyes widened at his announcement. I was bursting with excitement and a little pride at getting Conquest to back down. I didn't want to say anything that might make him change his mind, so I took a deep breath and spoke calmly, "Dinner you said. What did you have in mind?"

I followed him back to his house, guiding my bike alongside. Once we gathered the others, Liam led us around the house to the parking lot where many other college students parked their cars. We stopped in front of three motorcycles and I froze.

My heart raced in terror and anger at the machines in front of me. I used to love motorcycles, but my brother had died on one and I had burned the guys' motorcycles afterward. I suspected they replaced them, but I hadn't realized we would be riding on them today. I continued to stare in terror. Then again, there wasn't anything to actually be afraid of. My brother had been killed by Templars not a motorcycle. For a year I had been angry and afraid of the wrong thing.

I studied the three motorcycles looking for some reason I should say no. They were beautiful and each one a different shiny color. I took a deep breath deciding to give the vehicles another chance. All I had to do was tell myself they were not dangerous and try to move past my previous disposition. They were better than horses at least. I blinked, realizing the meanings of the colors and laughed.

"What are you laughing at?" Trevor asked going to the black bike and grabbing his helmet.

"I think she has finally gone crazy," Kaden muttered as he passed, going to stand by his red bike.

I looked to Liam with amusement, finally understanding his smile when he saw my bicycle earlier. Without meaning to I had chosen my Horseman color when I bought my bike. Liam offered me a helmet and guided me to the white motorcycle, the ride of Conquest, and started it up.

Getting on the back of a motorcycle brought back so many memories and feelings that I gasped at their intensity. Nervousness. Grief. Anger. Excitement. Liam must have sensed my tension and grabbed my hands, pulling my arms tighter around his midsection and then we were off. Liam led the way while Kaden and Trevor followed close behind.

At first, I stayed tensed, not having ridden in over a year. Then the wind and roaring of the engine soothed me and soon I was shouting my happiness into the air.

Oh yeah, I definitely preferred motorcycles over horses.

Chapter 8

We ended up stopping at a local diner, not too far from campus. I quirked an eyebrow at the theme. The diner was going for a post-apocalyptic theme with a Mad Max vibe and graffiti. Crazy outfits hung about, with spikes, masks, and grunge. There was even a wall full of knives. Before I could make fun of their choice, Liam grabbed my hand and pulled me over to a table.

I waited until we sat down and ordered before grilling them. "Were you serious about teaching me?" The guys looked everywhere except for me. I flung my foot out under the table and felt it connect with a solid, fleshy leg.

Kaden cursed and bent down to rub his leg, his eyes shooting daggers at me from across the table. I wasn't aiming for anyone specific but at least I got the attention of one of them. I sighed when they continued the silent treatment.

"Fine, I will just go then. Thanks for wasting my time." I made to stand up but Liam's hand on my shoulder stopped me from completing it.

"I said what I said," he grumbled.

I placed my elbow on the table and put my head in my hand, facing him. "So, what's first then?"

The waiter brought us a serving of bread and our drinks. The guys waited until he left before answering my question.

"A little history." Trevor grabbed a piece of bread, buttering it as he spoke. "How much do you know already?"

My cheeks reddened at my ignorance. "Only what the Bible says."

The guys nodded. "Not bad. It is not far off," Trevor replied, then stuffed the bread in his mouth preventing him from saying more.

"It took us a long time to figure everything out," Kaden added, making me feel a little better about my lack of knowledge.

"What we know so far is that the Horsemen have been around for thousands of years," Trevor added once he swallowed the food in his mouth. "Stories and art from all over the world depict some variety of the Horsemen. The Bible only made it popular."

I was shocked to hear that they had been around that long but surely, the guys were not actually that old. I was not over a thousand years old and my parents had baby pictures of me and Owen from eighteen years ago to prove it.”

My face must have shown my thoughts because Kaden chuckled. “We are not thousands of years old. Every time a set of Horsemen die, a new set are born and always in the order the Bible speaks of.”

I nodded, showing I understood. That was wild though. So, if all four of us died then a new set of Horsemen would be born starting with Conquest. I glanced at Liam wondering what his thoughts were, but he was a closed book.

“Around the Middle Ages, the Templars created an Order with the Pope’s guidance and set out to eliminate the Horsemen after they caused the black plague,” Trevor added.

I gasped. “The plague was the Horsemen?”

“And the Crusades too,” Liam said, finally participating in the history lesson. “Basically, anytime a major war or disease breaks out it is because of the Horsemen.”

I looked at the three of them horrified. I would never do anything like that. I never asked to be a Horseman. Even though the guys at that table were known to be violent sometimes I couldn’t believe any of them would do something like that either. “Is that why that Templar attacked me? Because he thinks I will start a war or pandemic?”

They nodded solemnly and I sat back trying to process that tidbit of information. Great, so I was going to have to watch my back for the rest of my life. How long did a Horseman last in such a world? I was too afraid to ask, especially after my brother was killed at only seventeen.

"Why are we being targeted though? I've read the Bible, I know it is the lamb that opens the seals. The Templars should find that lamb."

The guys stared at me dumbfounded then burst into laughter. I blew air into my cheeks and gave up that train of thought. Ok, it was a little ridiculous to blame a lamb but still, anything would be better than being hunted for something out of my control.

I would never do anything to bring the end of the world closer. If only there was some way to make the Templars believe that. However, history was on their side. I gasped as a thought struck me. "Is there any way to give up my role as a Horseman?"

They shook their head looking down at the table. "We've tried," Kaden said defeated.

I clenched my fists in anger, not ready to accept that I would be hunted forever. "Well there has to be a way to get them off our backs. We won't do anything crazy like past Horsemen did!"

I was shocked to see fear on their faces. Even Liam looked scared and I do not think I have ever seen him express that emotion. Then I realized why. "You guys think you might do something crazy, huh?"

"It's not like we want to. I would rather give all of this up," Kaden said angrily.

I nodded but waited for them to finish. I knew there was a but coming.

"But history shows that the Horsemen always cause some major world event. Always," Trevor said, sounding a bit exasperated.

"So, even if we don't want to cause a war or pandemic, something might happen accidentally someday." Liam threw the piece of bread he had in his hand onto his plate. "That's why I didn't want you to be part of this or learn anything about it."

The three of them wouldn't meet my eyes and the mood became depressing as we thought of what might happen. Then anger filled me again. I slammed my hand on the table causing them to jump and stare at me in confusion.

"I refuse to let anything happen." I turned to Liam, frustration obvious in the way I frowned at him. "If I don't learn who I am, and what I can do, then an accident will surely happen. Look at what happened at that party! It is better for me to know then randomly stumble upon it and hurt people." I now looked at the other two to make sure all three of them knew how serious I was. "I don't know what the past Horsemen thought or why they did those horrible things, but we are good people and the new generation, and we control what happens."

They stared at me with wide eyes. If they were going to say anything, they were interrupted by the waiter bringing our food. It was a pleasant way to bring us back to reality and I was grateful. I dug into my steak but paused when they continued staring at me. Trying to lighten the mood I decided for a joke. "You know, it's a surprise that no one has found you when you frequent a place having to do with the apocalypse. That's kinda holding up a flag saying *here I am*, isn't it?"

Kaden was the first to chuckle setting off Trevor in the process. Even Liam smiled and stopped staring at me, instead focusing on his prime rib. We stayed away from the Horsemen topic for the rest of dinner, which helped lighten the mood, but I still felt it hanging in the air. The diner had surprisingly good food. In my experience, diners that were heavily themed lacked tasty meals. However, my steak was delicious and from the way the guys ate, their food was equally good. Even Trevor's vegetarian dish looked yummy.

When we were finished, I attempted to add my card to pay for my meal, but Liam held up his hand. "I got it."

I wanted to argue but knowing Liam, I would get nowhere so instead I said thanks and put my card away. Once everything was wrapped up, I followed them out to the bikes. Suddenly, our situation was back in the forefront of our minds and tension thickened the air.

"Um, so what now?" I asked, swinging my arms by my sides feeling awkward.

Liam got onto his bike and held out a helmet to me. "Now we train you."

He started up the bike, making the engine roar. Trevor and Kaden did the same to theirs, but I continued standing on the sidewalk.

"Now?" I shouted over the engine. "It's late. I've got school tomorrow."

Liam quirked an eyebrow at me as if saying 'so you don't want to learn?'

After a moment of an intense stare down I grumbled and put the helmet on, getting on the back of Conquest's bike once more and letting him lead.

For now.

I made sure I had a list of questions ready when we got to their house, hoping to wring as much from them as I could before they clambered up again.

"You can take the guest room again," Kaden called over to me as we headed inside.

I nodded showing I heard him before making my way to the kitchen table and taking a seat. The others joined me, and I found myself amused that we unintentionally claimed that area as our meeting spot.

I didn't wait for them to change their mind. "How are you going to train me? How do I recognize a Templar? How did you guys discover your talents? Were you friends first or did this whole thing bring you together?"

I had more questions but the uneasy look on their faces prevented me from asking more. I would let them answer those first then continue.

Liam took his leather jacket off and pulled up the sleeve of his shirt showcasing a set of impressive muscles and a black tattoo of a bow and arrow.

I pressed my lips together and nodded with a frown, trying to convey I liked the tattoo but didn't understand what it had to do with my questions.

"Each of the Horsemen have a symbol and for some reason we have a talent for that particular weapon," Liam explained. "I am talented with a bow and arrow, Kaden is talented with a sword, and Trevor is talented with pretty much anything that will tip the scales in his favor."

I remembered seeing Trevor's tattoo of a set of scales, but I never realized their meaning. So, each of them had a tattoo of their Horseman symbol. Did that mean I would have to get one? I wasn't opposed to the idea, but I thought my first tattoo would have been a gear or a dragon.

"So, what is my weapon?"

It was Trevor who answered by laying it on the kitchen table. I hadn't even seen him get up let alone leave the room long enough to grab it. A long pole, the size of my arm, ended in a curved blade. It looked old and used.

"A scythe?" I mentally facepalmed. I should have known. Death was like the Grim Reaper. Did that mean I could reap souls? "I am going to train with a scythe. Won't it look weird carrying it around school?"

The others chuckled. "You're not going to carry it around. This is the original scythe used by the first Horseman," Liam explained.

My eyes widened and I stared at the weapon with new interest. Then I wrinkled my nose. "Won't it break then?"

They ignored my question and decided to answer the first ones I asked. "There are not many ways to identify a Templar," Kaden said. "Usually their crest gives them away seeing as how they are very prideful of their Order."

I assumed the crest was a cross with a sword since the maniac in the library wore it. I feel like I had seen the crest elsewhere before but couldn't remember where. Well, if I ever saw it, I would run the other way. That may make me sound like a chicken, but I did not want to be stabbed.

"As for the other two questions, I don't really feel like sharing my personal business with you," Liam said in a cold tone standing up and dismissing the meeting.

I glared at him. He didn't have to answer all my questions, but he didn't have to be a jerk about it either.

"You will stay here tonight. We will start your weapon and talent training after classes tomorrow." Liam didn't wait for a response. He left the kitchen and I heard him stomp up the stairs.

I turned to the other two. "What got his panties in a twist?"

They held their hands up and shrugged in the universal sign of *I don't know* but avoided my gaze. Fine, I will find out later. I touched the scythe on the table and sighed. It will be a long time before I accepted that I was Death. I left Kaden and Trevor at the table while I trudged up the stairs, texting Shawna about my plans to stay. I should go back to my dorm, but I was tired. Stopping in the bathroom first I decided to take a long, hot shower. The warm water soaked through to my bones until all the tension drained from my body. I didn't know how long I was in there, but my pruning fingers told me long enough.

I shut the water off and got out of the shower, only realizing then that I didn't have any clean clothes. I looked to the towel rack and noticed a couple wrinkled towels. Eww. I wasn't about to use one of the guys' towels to dry off or wrap myself in. I rifled through the cabinets searching for a new towel so I could go to the guest room and figure out my clothes situation. Finally, I found a stack and reached for the top one only to freeze as a bottle next to it caught my eye.

My hand drifted to the bottle instead and pulled it from the cabinet. Then my mind started to spin. They had chloroform in their bathroom. The morning after the party my roommate told me I was brought home by the guys since I passed out from being drunk. However, the bottle in my hand proved that my dream was true. They had drugged me. I should have remembered that tidbit sooner but better late than never. Rage filled my body. I had the decency of mind to grab a clean towel to wrap around me before I stormed from the bathroom and into Liam's bedroom, clenching the bottle of chloroform.

He looked up from his desk surprised and his eyes flitted down my semi naked body. My cheeks began to warm under his heated gaze, but I forced my myself to remember why I was there. I held out the bottle accusingly making his eyes narrow. He crossed his arms and sat back in his desk chair comfortably. Anger filled me again at his casual demeanor.

"You drugged me!" He didn't answer which only enraged me further. I stalked over to him and pointed my finger in his face. "You trapped me in a closet then when I thought you were letting me go you drugged me," I accused through gritted teeth.

Liam had the audacity to smile. That was the last straw. I opened my palm and swung at his face. Suddenly my wrist was held in a tight grip and I was yanked forward into a hard chest. I tried to pull away, but an arm wrapped around my back caging me in. The hand that wasn't being held continued gripping the bottle of chloroform and I was tempted to toss it at Liam's head to make him let go but the angle was all wrong and I would have ended up dropping it instead.

"You don't know what happened that night," Liam growled in a low voice. Gruffness was written all over his face, but his eyes held desire and amusement. The mix of emotions coming from him confused me, but I didn't let it change the fact that I was pissed.

I narrowed my eyes at him. "There is no excuse for using this on me," I said in just as low a voice and shook the bottle in my hand.

"After you killed that man, Templars showed up. I shoved you in the closet to keep you safe while we dealt with them. Then I thought the best course of action was making you forget everything and keep you from freaking out. Hence the chloroform."

He said it so casually that for a moment I was thrown. Oh yeah, we were just having a party, you know, then fought some people and then drugged our late best friend's sister. No biggie. I shook my head and yanked at my arm again and bared my teeth like a wolf. I was going for dangerous, but I probably looked like a lunatic.

"You could have just talked to me like a normal person!"

Before Liam could say anything, Kaden knocked on the open door. "Um, is everything alright?"

I craned my neck to see him, difficult though it was, and saw Kaden and Trevor with concerned looks darting from Liam to me who he still had trapped against him. Abruptly Liam let go and I nearly fell backwards but righted myself at the last moment. I was surprised my towel stayed on. Thank you, universe.

Liam spun his chair around to sit facing away from us. Trevor had his hands partially raised as if he wanted to catch me or pull me away or something. I just shook my head at him and scowled at the two of them. They were just as guilty. I saw a familiar bag in Kaden's hand and knew they had gone to get me clothes and other essentials. I stormed towards them, grabbed my bag forcefully from him and started to leave. It bothered me how calm Liam was about drugging me. At the last second, I ran to Liam's bed, grabbed a pillow, and tossed it at Liam's head. I wanted to elicit a reaction other than his annoying calmness.

Liam shouted, but I ran from the room and into the guest bedroom before he could reach me. I quickly locked the door and leaned against it. Tears burned my eyes. I had been so vulnerable that night at the party and it irked me how comfortable Liam was with what he did. I held up the bottle in my hand staring at it with determination then opened my bag and stuffed the bottle inside.

We would see how comfortable he was when it was me drugging him. I know, I know, that doesn't make me any better than him, but hey, I never claimed to be a better person.

Chapter 9

I made sure I was out of the house before they woke. I wanted to get breakfast with Shawna then get to my classes so I could glare daggers at each of the guys when they walked in. I was still royally pissed at their actions, but I knew I still had to meet up with them later to train.

Shawna met me with a huge grin and hugged me. I let out a grunt from the tight squeeze but hugged her back, glad that at least one person in my life hadn't hurt me.

When she pulled back, she waggled her eyebrows. "So, tell me about last night."

I rolled my eyes and moved past her and handed over my ID to the lady near the door so she could swipe it and let me in to the dining area. Shawna followed closely.

"That bad?" she asked. "You know, I don't understand why you stay over there when you don't like them." She bumped me with her hip. "I could always go with you next time."

I stopped and stared at her with a raised eyebrow. "Which one is on your radar?" I asked knowing why she suggested going over there.

Shawna sighed, and walked over to the closest food buffet. "Kaden is smokin' hot and funny don't you think?"

I wrinkled my nose. "Meh." I smiled thinking about how Kaden would have given a dramatic pout about my meh comment. He was good looking just like the other two, but I didn't think of Kaden that way. "Good luck." I grabbed a plate of food and led us to a table nearby.

"It will happen one of these days, it is inevitable," Shawna said with surety before taking a bite of her scrambled eggs. "So, I was thinking of joining some clubs."

I was startled by the change of subject but grateful. "What kind of clubs?"

She shrugged. "I haven't decided yet. Would you like to join some with me?"

I beamed at the idea, but my smile immediately died with the realization I wouldn't have time if I was going to train every day. I pouted down at my food. "Maybe next semester."

Shawna gave me a half smile. "Well, I will let you know how they go then."

I was the worst friend. I barely hung out with her and the one time I agreed to go somewhere with her I had ended up unconscious. She probably thought I was avoiding her. I vowed then and there to spend more time with my roommate because without her I might just go insane.

We talked about our classes for the rest of breakfast and the projects we were working on. It was nice to talk about something besides the guys and think of something other than Horsemen business. I was also grateful because she reminded me of a project that was due in Engineering that I had completely forgotten about. I would have to find time to do it before the end of the week.

After classes I made my way to the house where the guys said they would meet me for training. I was both nervous and excited to start swinging around a scythe and knock them on their butts. Imagining Liam on the floor after I swiped his legs made me smile. My smile died when three sets of frowning gazes met me once I reached the house.

"I am not staying tonight so let's get this over with," I told them, trying not to show how excited I was to train or how upset I was for being drugged by them. My new goal was to show indifference from here on out.

Liam led the way inside. The first thing I noticed was the open living room, devoid of furniture. In place of the couch and tv was a large mat which I had seen in gyms before for wrestling and gymnastics. Liam continued into the house, and up the stairs, leaving the rest of us in the living room. I stared after him with a mix of confusion and annoyance. Was he not going to stay? Whatever.

"The first hour we will work on fighting and defense. The second hour will be talent training," Kaden explained as he passed me to stand on the mat. He waved me over and positioned me in the middle.

I've punched someone before, even though it was my brother, but it counted. I would totally ace this training. I quickly threw my backpack to the side, tied my hair back into a braid, then bent my knees a bit and brought my fists up in front of me. Kaden would be surprised by how well I could defend myself. I watched him, waiting for the first move but he only smirked. Something heavy suddenly slammed into me from the side and I fell with a whoosh of breath.

Trevor stood over me with his arms crossed and a huge grin on his face. "First rule. Be aware of your surroundings."

I clenched my jaw at their obvious humor over my lack of skills, but I didn't say anything. Instead choosing to hang on to indifference. I got back up and positioned myself, so I was facing both of them. This time it was Kaden who charged me but instead of facing him fully like I knew Trevor wanted I stepped back and stuck my foot out. Kaden saw it just in time and did a little hop dance to avoid it. Using his poor balance against him, I stepped forward and tapped his chest, making him fall into Trevor.

"Ok, you got lucky on that one," Kaden grumbled, righting himself.

For the next hour, we practiced offensive moves and defensive ones. I found that, yes, I can indeed punch but doing it repeatedly hurt. I was a sweating, heavy breathing, lump of dead muscle by the end. So much for indifference. The annoying part was that Kaden and Trevor seemed unfazed by the exertion.

"So-" I took a deep breath trying to get my breathing under control. "So, when do we fight with weapons?"

Trevor smiled but it was Kaden who answered. "When you're ready," he chuckled.

I waved my hand at them and let it flop back to the mat where I lay. "Pshh, I'm totally ready."

"Mhm," Trevor sounded disbelievingly. He held out a hand and I grasped it, letting him pull me into an upright position. Trevor then gave me a wave and walked up the stairs to his room. I glanced from the stairs to Kaden wondering about Trevor's departure, but he waved my silent question away. I guessed this next part was only a two-person thing.

Kaden sat down, cross legged, in front of me. "Now for talent training."

Suddenly, nerves wracked my body. This was something I needed to do to get better control, but I was terrified of what harm I could cause. "I'm Death, right? Maybe we shouldn't practice." I bit my lip imagining black boils erupting over Kaden and shivered.

He laid a hand on my arm. "Don't worry, you can't kill me. We may be able to cause emotional disturbances in each other, but we cannot kill each other."

I calmed a bit at that knowledge. I was still skeptical, but I figured he knew what he was talking about. "Ok, let's do this."

"First, let me show you what I can do and how I control it. We may find that your control is the same." He reached out and touched my arm.

At first nothing happened, and I started to ask what was supposed to happen when my hand suddenly came up and slapped him in the face. I put a hand over my gaping mouth in horror.

He withdrew his touch and held a hand to his face. I thought he would be mad, but he looked amused.

"I am *so* sorry Kaden. I don't know why I did that," I rushed to say.

He chuckled. "I do. What did you feel right before that?"

I frowned trying to remember. At first, I was confused because nothing was happening but then a strong current of anger rushed through me and I needed to retaliate. I gasped at the realization. "You made me angry!"

He nodded. "Right. Anger often leads to war which is why that is my talent."

I looked at him in wonder. "Can you teach me that?"

He shook his head. "You will not be able to cause anger. Death's specialty is illness and loss."

He reached forward and touched my arm again making me tense. I was determined this time to be aware of the anger and control it. I focused on his touch waiting for the inevitable.

"First we start with a touch, then I focus on what makes me angry and imagine pushing that through my arm and into the person I am touching." With that, a burst of simmering heat filled my chest and I gritted my teeth. I wanted to slap him again, but I refrained. "With a few words, I can use your anger to target others." Another burst of anger raged through me but before I could lash out at him, he whispered, "I can't believe Trevor thought you were weak."

Suddenly I was up and storming toward the stairs. That Horseman was in for a treat. I would show him how strong I really was. Only when I reached the bottom step did I freeze and realize what Kaden did. Dang he was good. Even when he warned me he was going to do it I still reacted to the false anger. I turned around embarrassed and made my way back to the mat where Kaden sat smirking.

"Do you always have to touch someone?" Memories of the library incident came to mind. Liam didn't need to touch the Templar to send him running in fear.

Kaden bobbed his head. "It depends. Most of the time yes, but under extreme circumstances when our own emotions are running high, we can project them. However, it takes enormous energy."

I nodded slowly. That means Liam was extremely emotional that night. That made me warm inside to know he cared. Not that he would ever admit it.

"Now your turn."

I bit my lip nervously and reached out. I touched Kaden's knee with the tips of my fingers, but I didn't know how to continue. Seeing my struggle Kaden advised, "Just think of making me feel sick."

I imagined my stomach roiling and head spinning with fever. Then I imagined pushing those feelings out of my hand to Kaden. After a couple minutes, Kaden grabbed my fingers and moved them away from him, breaking my connection.

"That was decent. My stomach was a little upset, and I am fairly sure my head began to feel fuzzy. Maybe. But it was not nearly strong enough to do any damage. Try again."

For the rest of the hour we practiced using our talents on each other. I did not make much progress because I could not figure out the trigger to make the emotion strong. Kaden called it a night around eight and I stood up groaning from stiff muscles. I needed a hot shower and a good night's rest. Two sets of footsteps bounded down the stairs until Liam and Trevor stood before us.

"You're staying here tonight," Liam ordered.

I scoffed at his authority. What gave him the right to boss me around? He better not think that since I was a

Horseman he had control over me. "No." I grabbed my backpack and walked toward the door.

Liam was suddenly there, holding it closed with his palm. "You need to stay here where it is safe. I overheard your training. You're not ready to protect yourself."

I rolled my eyes. He didn't want to help train me, but he was fine judging from upstairs? "I will be fine." I turned to Kaden and Trevor. "Tell him I will be fine."

"Well-" Kaden started.

"Go upstairs," Liam said, cutting Kaden off, and kept his eyes trained on me.

I quirked a brow and crossed my arms, refusing to move. I knew trying to remove his hand from the door would be fruitless, so I waited. When I didn't move after a minute of our intense stare down, Liam grabbed my upper arm and started to drag me toward the stairs. I protested but nothing I said would make him let go. I reached into my backpack and pulled out my pepper spray. I had gotten a can after the library incident. Before he knew what I planned, I jumped in front of him and sprayed his face.

He abruptly let go and wiped at his face as he shouted in pain. I felt a twinge of regret, but I used the moment to dart away from him and to the door. I left Kaden and Trevor laughing hysterically and Liam cursing me. I knew he would get his revenge but for tonight I had won. See? I could protect myself just fine. I hopped onto my bike and sped back to my dorm.

Shawna was at her desk with books and papers laid out when I walked in. She beamed at me and stood up from her desk. "Nice to see you! What have you been up to?"

"I pepper sprayed Liam," I said with a straight face then threw my bag on my desk chair. There was no way I would get any work done tonight. My phone buzzed constantly but I ignored it, not wanting to read the angry messages from Liam. I was starting to regret adding his number to my phone.

"You what?" Shawna shouted. Then anger tinged her tone, "What did he do to you? Do I need to pummel him?

I chuckled, the anger from a few moments ago seeping from my body. I walked over to her and gave her a bear hug. The breath whooshed from her, but she hugged me back.

"Thanks," I said against her shoulder.

"For what?" she chuckled.

"Thanks for being willing to beat up people for me." We both laughed at my words and I pulled back. "I'll be back, I'm going to go take a shower, then we can hang out and talk for the rest of the night."

Shawna nodded and sat at her desk again while I grabbed my shower stuff. I was glad to have at least one friend who didn't try to control me and who wanted to hang out with me for me and not because I was a Horseman.

Chapter 10

The rest of the weeks went by in a blur. If I wasn't training, I was in classes, and if I wasn't in classes or training, I was doing projects in my dorm. I hated that the sanctuary of the library had been ruined for me but until I found a new quiet place, the dorm it was. I was enjoying all my classes, especially Engineering Design. Shawna was often at her club meetings in the evenings and occasionally on outings during the weekends. We had found some time to do stuff together though which I was grateful for. Thankfully I had no more run ins with Templars, and I had avoided Liam like the plague. Haha, plague. I was more likely the one to cause that.

The other two Horsemen I did not mind much and had even grown closer to them. I considered them friends now, but it always got awkward when Liam was around. Maybe if he got off his high horse then we could make peace but until then awkward it would be.

Knocking sounded at my door and I rose from my chair to answer it curiously. I did not know many people and Shawna did not need to knock. I opened the door cautiously and two sets of beaming smiles met me.

"Mom? Dad?" I asked though I could see it was obviously them. I stepped back to let them in, wondering how they even got into the building. Did speaker boy let them in without an ID? I really had to find that guy.

My mom sprang forward and crushed me in a tight hug. She had on a yellow and brown poncho and her brown hair was styled short. "Oh, we missed you! How are classes? Is your roommate nice?"

I had answered those same questions on the phone last week. I wondered what caused them to come all the way to Penn State without notice. "Um, yeah she's great. Not that I don't love seeing you, but uh, why are you guys here?" I pulled back and hugged my dad in greeting.

He kept his hair short and his round glasses and suspenders reminded me of 1920s fashion. He loved wearing historical styles. "Honey, don't you remember? It's parents' weekend! We told you last week we were coming."

I mentally facepalmed. I completely forgot. Well, I guess I was stuck with them. Not that I minded. I loved them but I was always on edge when they were around, wondering what kind of mood they would be in. Ever since Owen's death, they had become morose and a bit unstable. It was hard to gauge their mood most times. For now, they seemed happy but that could change in an instant.

"Right, I remember." I stood there and fidgeted with my Hawaiian bracelet. "So, what do you want to do?"

"Show us around. We want to see everything," my mom said smiling.

I took my parents to each of the buildings where my classes were located, to the dining area, and passed the library. There was not much else to show them unless I wanted to take them to see Liam, Kaden, and Trevor which I did not. As far as my parents knew, I had not seen those three in a year. No need to open old wounds.

My phone buzzed and I pulled it out to see a text from Shawna. Perfect timing. I texted her back to meet us at the wing take-out place then led my parents there. They were excited to meet the person I had been living with over the past couple of months. I wondered if I would meet Shawna's family today. She hadn't mentioned they were coming but then again maybe she had, and I just forgot. My mind has been a bit occupied lately.

I didn't see Shawna yet when we arrived, so we went ahead and ordered and found a seat to wait. My parents gushed over the beauty of campus and told me stories about their new gardening hobby and how they were hoping for vegetables soon so they could send me some.

A few minutes later, Shawna found us, her presence halting my dad's story about the vegetables they planted. "Hi! I'm Shawna!" She held her food in one hand and held out her other hand for my parents to shake in greeting.

My dad, ever the gentleman, stood and pulled out a chair for her to sit in after he shook her hand. My mom greeted her next. "I hope our Ophelia hasn't been causing too much trouble," she said.

I rolled my eyes. They knew all too well I was not the type to cause trouble.

Shawna laughed and shook her head. "Not at all, Mrs. Bronson."

My dad looked around before bringing his attention back to Shawna. "Are your parents here?"

Shawna tensed briefly then relaxed making me think I imagined it. "No, not this time. They are currently in Italy schmoozing with the Pope."

"The Pope!" My mother exclaimed excitedly.

"Italy!" My father exclaimed at the same time. "That must be nice."

Shawna shrugged, keeping her focus on her food. "Eh, not really, they travel a lot on business, so it is not like a vacation or anything."

My father nodded as if he knew what she was talking about, but I would bet he was curious what kind of business let them travel to Italy often. His own job had to do with international finances but even he did not get to travel.

"Anyway, I heard something about gardening when I walked up," Shawna said, changing the subject in true Shawna fashion.

The way her smile tightened, and shoulders tensed made me think she did not have a good relationship with her parents. My heart ached for her. Even though mine could have crazy mood swings, I still valued the relationship I had with them. I wanted to ask her about it but wasn't sure if our friendship was at the point where I could. I hadn't even told her about my brother yet.

My parents took the change of subject in stride and talked for the rest of our meal about their new garden, occasionally asking us about our Engineering projects. I found myself relaxed and happy for the first time in a while. I had missed my parents and loved how they could be so excited about everything despite being depressed much of the time. I was eager to finish my Engineering project so I could send them pictures and show off my skills now that they showed interest.

Once our conversation fell into a lull, Shawna stood and grabbed her trash. "Well, I will leave you guys alone now. It was nice meeting you."

My dad sighed and stood up as well. "Actually, we should get going. We will have to come back soon and visit you two again."

My mom and I stood to join them and the four of us disposed of our trash then met outside. We stood in a circle for an awkward moment before my dad moved in and hugged me. I held him tight knowing it would be a while before I saw him again. They did not leave home much these days. They hadn't even left to drop me off at college. My mom moved in next and grabbed Shawna along the way to bring her in for a group hug. Shawna looked surprised but accepted the hug.

"They seem like nice people," Shawna said once they left.

I nodded. "They are." I turned to Shawna with hesitation. "So, your parents are in Italy, huh?"

Her eyes moved to the ground in between us. "Yeah, they have been there for a couple weeks. They are in charge of expanding a program to other parts of the world."

I wanted to ask her about it, but she didn't seem to want to talk about her parents, so I let it drop. "So, what do you want to do now?"

She looked relieved. "I don't know, I was going to go do some homework."

I needed to do homework too, but I wanted to spend more time with my friend. Between training and her clubs, we hadn't seen much of each other. "Want to go see a movie?"

Shawna's face brightened. "Yes!"

I hadn't been to the theater in that town yet and found it was only a bus ride away. I could have ridden my bike there, but Shawna did not have one so the bus it was. I was pleasantly surprised to see the theater was not busy which allowed us to get our snacks and seats quickly.

Shawna bounced in her seat and talked nonstop until the movie started. I had not laughed that much in a long time and was happy to have spent some time with my new friend. Halfway through the movie though my bladder screamed at me. I should have gone to the bathroom before it started but I was too focused on getting our seats and talking.

I told Shawna I would be back then made my way out to an empty bathroom. Thank goodness a movie hadn't let out yet otherwise the bathroom would have had a line. I finished my business and was washing my hands when a loud noise made me jump. I glanced in the mirror to see behind me and found a girl with blonde hair and blue eyes staring at me with disgust. I had seen her before. She was the smoothie murderer.

I turned around to face her completely. The crest on her jacket sent a spike of fear through me but I kept my expression calm. I knew I had seen that crest elsewhere before. So far, I did not see any swords so that was a plus.

"Excuse me," I said trying to pass her and leave the bathroom to the lobby where there would be witnesses. She would not try to kill me if there were witnesses around. Right?

She grabbed my shoulder roughly and yanked me back, making me stumble into the sink. "You don't deserve to live," the girl said in a low, angry voice.

I gaped at her. She didn't even know me.

"I told you the next time I saw you, you would regret it." She advanced toward me while a dagger slipped out of her jacket sleeve and into her open palm where she grabbed it and swung the sharp end toward me. It was such a smooth motion that I almost didn't process its existence in time.

If she wasn't about to kill me, I would have stopped to admire the trick. Instead I dove for the side, feeling a sting in my shoulder. I touched the spot where pain radiated from, and my fingers came away coated in blood. A scream stuck in my throat as she came at me again. This time I used my defensive strategies that Kaden taught me and side stepped the blade then punched her in the face.

She rocked backward, her hand going up to hold her jaw. Rage filled her eyes and a very nasty word left her lips. I had been called that before but, in this instance, it only made me smirk because it meant I had gotten to her. She swiped out at me again causing me to back up or be stabbed. I was really getting tired of being attacked with sharp weapons. I had to start carrying a knife of my own. Too bad I left my purse in the theater or else I could pull out my pepper spray.

Despite my moves to disarm her or defend myself she got another hit in leaving my hand sliced open. I hissed at the pain as red stained my palm. The pain from my hand and shoulder filled me, making me angry. That maniac had been able to hurt me twice. If I didn't do something soon, someone would find me lying dead in a bathroom. Not exactly the way I wanted to go.

The rage built until I felt I would burst. When the girl attacked me again, I ignored the pain and stepped into her attack. I leaned to the side so the blade could glide past then I grabbed her neck with my bloody hand. I pushed all my fury, despair, and fear that she made me feel out. Her body went slack and eyes wide. The blade dropped and black boils erupted over her skin. Suddenly horrified I dropped my hand and watched her crumple.

Shit. Shit. Shit.

There were not as many boils or black patches on her as the last person I unintentionally killed but she was still writhing on the floor and whimpering. At least now I knew that anger and fear had a part in activating my powers. I used her distraction as an advantage and rushed out of the bathroom, grabbing some paper towels on the way out to press against my bloody palm. A boy behind the counter looked up as I burst out of the bathroom and must have seen something in my eyes. He hurried around the counter and reached out to me asking if I was alright. I waved him away and pointed to the bathroom.

"Someone collapsed in there, call 911." His eyes widened and he rushed to do as I said.

While he was distracted, I went back into the theater where Shawna sat watching the movie, completely oblivious to the fact that I just fought someone with pestilence.

Shawna smiled at me when I reached her and whispered, "Hey, you missed a great part. The main charac-"

I cut her off by grabbing my stuff and pulling on her hand. "I need to go."

Her smile dropped and she followed me out. "What's wrong?"

I thanked her mentally for not arguing and instead going along with my sudden need to leave. I ignored her question and pulled out my phone, sending a quick text to Liam. I knew I could have contacted Trevor or Kaden, but I felt Liam was the person I needed right now.

Shawna pulled on my hand that was still grasping hers to stop me when we left the building. "Phi, what's wrong? Are you ok?"

I put my phone away after reading Liam's reply that they were on their way. Shawna noticed my injured hand and gasped. "Oh my God, Phi! What happened?"

I shook my head, not wanting to tell her the truth. "I fell in the bathroom and sliced my hand on something sharp. I'm not feeling great, so I want to go. I'm sorry, if you want to stay you can."

Shawna eyed me with suspicion and worry. Then she saw my shoulder and reached out to touch it hovering just above the cut. "You fell and hurt yourself twice?"

I hesitated. "No, same fall, two places got hurt." I cringed knowing that sounded unbelievable.

"We should get you to a hospital," Shawna said, tugging me to the bus stop.

I pulled on her hand this time and she stopped, turning to me with worry shining in her eyes. "I'm fine, it is just a couple of small cuts."

Shawna eyed my hand like it might fall off, but she didn't argue.

Three roaring engines sounded behind us and I turned to see Liam, Kaden, and Trevor riding up to the curb near us. Tension I hadn't realized I held dissipated at seeing them. They made me feel safe. Liam took his helmet off and rushed over to me, cradling my hand in his. I stiffened at the contact but if he noticed, he didn't show it.

"Why are you guys here?" Shawna asked bewildered, looking behind Liam to the other two.

Liam gave me a knowing look but flashed Shawna a boyish smile. "She texted saying you two needed a ride home."

Shawna raised her brows and looked to me with a silent question. I knew she was wondering whether I actually texted Liam and whether I was ok with going with them since I often showed my dislike of them. Little did she know I had been training with the guys and growing fond of them over the past few weeks. I nodded and she sighed.

"Ok." Then she beamed. "I call riding with Kaden!" She ran to the red motorcycle and hopped on the back, squeezing Kaden from behind who smiled at my friend flirtatiously.

I winced at the sudden stinging in my palm and looked down to see Liam wrapping my hand in a bandage. Then he moved on to my shoulder and patched that up. He was so gentle and for once he was not lecturing me or scowling at my actions. His arm wrapped around my shoulders when he finished and tucked me into his side. It made me feel warm and safe, and I had to fight to keep blood from rushing to my cheeks.

He looked down at me with concern. "Are you ok? Tell me what happened."

I glanced at Shawna. Even though she wouldn't be able to hear me over the roaring of the motorcycle engines and her fascination with Kaden I still shook my head. "Later."

He nodded once, then led me to his motorcycle. This was the second time I would be riding on a motorcycle. I stood in front of the bike waiting for the usual fear to fill me, but this time I was calm. Yay, progress. I smiled at that and got on the back, accepting the helmet Liam held out.

Back on campus, Kaden broke away to drop Shawna off at our dorm while Trevor and Liam continued to their house. As soon as we were inside, Liam led me to the unofficial meeting spot at the kitchen table and handed me a glass of water. My hands shook as I took it.

"What happened," Liam asked, sitting across from me.

Trevor took the other seat next to Liam and both of them stared at me with varying degrees of concern and anger. At first, I thought they were angry at me but when Trevor glanced at my bandaged hand, I realized they were angry that someone hurt me.

"I was attacked by a Templar in the bathroom. She came at me with a knife, but I was able to block most of her attacks." I gulped, not wanting to continue. I wondered what happened to her.

"How did you get away?" Trevor asked. His hand was clenched so tightly his knuckles turned white and his anger was palpable. I could feel my stomach clench in the beginnings of hunger and my heart ached softly with despair, but I knew it was because I was picking up on Trevor's talent that he was exuding.

I bit my lip, not wanting to answer. "I think I killed her with pestilence."

I expected them to get mad about my talent killing someone again, but they showed no emotion. Not even grief over a person's death.

Their lack of emotion irked me. "Don't you care that I killed another person?" Grief slammed into me and I closed my eyes for a moment to reel it in. Even though she had attacked to kill I still felt bad about her death.

"No," Liam said.

I sat back in shock. "No?"

Liam leaned forward to fill the space I left behind. "No. It was kill or be killed."

I was stunned by his opinion. Trevor's impassive face told me he thought the same. Surely there could have been another way. I needed to control my powers, so I didn't keep killing people.

After a few moments of silence, I whispered, "Have you ever killed anyone?"

Liam stared at me with an intensity I didn't understand. In that instance I could see the line between human and supernatural and it frightened me. It was possible the emotions rolling off him caused my fear since that was his talent.

Before he could answer, Kaden walked through the door with a loud greeting. "Hey! Your roommate is all cozy in her room, wondering about you." His smile dropped when he saw our somber expressions. "What'd I miss?"

Liam got up from his chair and stalked up the stairs without a backward glance. I sighed. Someone touched my arm and I jumped. Trevor. I had almost forgotten he was still there.

"We have all killed people. We are not proud of it, but it has kept us safe." With that he too got up and walked upstairs.

I could not imagine Trevor, Liam, or Kaden killing anyone but then again, I had never imagined I could either.

Chapter 11

Kaden walked me home after I refused to stay the night at their place. I didn't see Trevor or Liam again before I left, and Kaden had grown quiet since interrupting the conversation earlier. Kaden waved when we reached my dorm and left me to go inside alone. Shawna pounced on me as soon as I went into the room and squeezed me in a hug.

I grunted at the pain in my shoulder and she released me looking apologetic. "Sorry. So, are you going to tell me what really happened?"

I knew she wouldn't believe the story about me falling but I couldn't tell her the truth. "It's nothing you have to worry about, I'm fine now."

Shawna stared at me with varying degrees of worry, exasperation, and relief. I moved past her, breaking eye contact and laid my purse by my desk.

"Did someone hurt you?" Shawna whispered.

I froze, my back facing her. Then I turned plastering a smile on my face to hide the fear and anger I had felt in the bathroom of the theater. "Nope."

Shawna stood there a moment longer then sighed, realizing I wouldn't say more. I hoped this didn't fracture the friendship we had forming. I could understand if she was hurt but I didn't want to lose her trust in me. Shawna's phone rang from her desk and the screen lit up displaying the caller as her dad. Shawna grumbled and grabbed the phone, telling me she would be back soon, before leaving the room.

Once alone, I let the hurt come over me and rolled my shoulder trying to get the ache out. My hand did not feel any better which would make it difficult to do my Engineering projects. Stupid Templars. This was the second time I had been attacked by one of them. Unfortunately, I was ninety-nine percent sure there would be a next time. Today it was my hand and shoulder that got hurt but what would happen next? I could not stay sane if I had to watch my back all the time. I knew training would only get me so far. Being a badass Horseman had not stopped the Templars from killing my brother.

Thinking about what happened to my brother and subsequently me made my body shake with anger and despair. I crumpled, feeling it all overwhelm me.

"Owen!" I cried out. "Why did you have to leave! This is all your fault!"

I knew that wasn't fair. He had no more control over our lives than the others did and even less now that he was dead. I wish I could just talk to him and learn about being Death from him. The others were used to living as the Horsemen but none of them knew what it was like to be Death. All they had to worry about was controlling emotions, but I had to worry about spreading disease and killing people with a touch. Did Owen have to go through the same thing? I gritted my teeth trying to reign in my frustration.

Phi, don't cry.

I jerked up at the voice that shouldn't be there. My tears stopped and adrenaline flooded my body. Someone was in my room and it wasn't Shawna. "Who's there?" I called out feeling ridiculous. I looked around but no one was in sight. Great, now I was hearing voices. I wiped at my face and pulled myself together.

I know it's tough, but you can get through this.

I froze on my way to bed and looked around again. No one was there but I knew that voice. I shook my head, trying to make my mind stop imagining things. That's just what everyone needs. A hallucinating Horseman.

I crawled up to my bed above my desk and plopped facedown into my pillows. "Go away," I told the voice. I chuckled thinking about what Shawna would do if she heard me talking to thin air.

Trust them.

I lifted my head to glare at my room. The universe was being cruel right now. I was already hurt but now it was making me imagine my brother's voice too. My heart clenched, wanting to see him so badly.

A flicker of light followed by an almost transparent face flittered in front of me. I screamed and rolled off my bed, righting myself in time before my face crashed into my desk chair below.

The light did not disappear, instead taking form and clearing to show a healthy and happy Owen. My breath caught at the sight of him. "Owen?"

I could see the other side of the room through him, but his body was still visible. "Oh my God. I can see you! Are you actually here or am I imagining this?"

Owen chuckled and stepped toward me. "I'm really here."

He looked exactly like he did before he died. Floppy black hair with a white streak, round face and freckles around his nose. For the first time I saw a scythe tattoo marking the inside of his left arm. Had he always had that?

"That's what a mirage would say," I said breathlessly. It was like old times, joking with my twin but this time he was a ghost and I was apparently insane.

"I heard you call out to me," Owen said softly, flicking his eyes around me then lingering on my injured hand. His face contorted in silent fury then smoothed into one of pain and regret. "I'm so sorry you got dragged into this."

I shook my head. I knew I blamed him before, but I hadn't meant it. "How are you here?" I asked happily. I would accept this vision of my brother as real until someone locked me in an insane asylum.

He shook his head as if to say he didn't know but a wide grin broke out on his face. Pure joy radiated from him until I felt my previous worries fall away. "I have no idea. I heard you and it was as if I was being pulled through a light until I arrived here. I saw you crying."

"Yeah, I kinda broke. This Horsemen stuff is endangering my life and I keep killing people." I shook my head in exasperation and sat in my desk chair. Owen leaned down and reached for me, but his hand hovered an inch above mine. "I know how you feel. It was difficult for me at first."

"How did you get through it?" I had discovered anger and desperation worked best for bringing out deathly diseases but anything else evaded me.

"Well, I used my fists. A lot," Owen laughed.

I chuckled at the memories. "Yeah you guys were kind of known as fists-first-words-later guys. You know you didn't have to go fight everyone in the school." My brother was extremely kind and funny but often put up a wall around strangers. When he got involved with Liam and the others, Owen had turned into a jerk of sorts, always getting into fights. The four of them had created a reputation.

Owen scrunched his nose. "It's not what it seems. Most of those people we beat up," he put air quotes around beat up, "were Templars. Except Johnny Marks. He was just a punk who needed to be put in his place." My eyes widened at the declaration. "Templars show up wherever the Horseman are. I had to learn early on how to fight and how no one was who they seemed." Owen frowned. "Do not trust anyone except Liam, Trevor and Kaden," he warned.

I wanted to argue that they were not the only people I could trust but I stayed quiet. No need to get him riled up about who I could and could not hang out with. I already had enough of that from Liam.

"Yeah but they got you in the end." Sadness filled every word and hung heavy in the air as I reminded myself he was a ghost right now.

"That they did. There's no changing that. But they will not get you."

Sighing in annoyance, I glared at my ghost brother. "You can't know that."

"No, but we can make it that way. Let the guys protect you."

I rolled my eyes at that. I knew they could protect me, but I did not necessarily want to rely on them. Plus, Liam's moods changed too much. I never knew what he thought of me and there was no way I would be a burden.

"Another thing you need to do is learn to access your other talents. When I was alive, I could make people feel sick. Have you tried that?"

I've tried making Kaden feel sick, but it never worked as well as their talents. "How do I do that without killing?"

"The key is to remember what death feels like."

I was about to ask him how I would know what death felt like if I had never died but my dorm room door opened, and Shawna walked in. I glanced to Owen wondering what I was going to say to explain my twin in ghost form, but he was gone. My heart clenched, and tears pricked my eyes.

He was gone. Again.

Shawna sat in her chair and threw her phone onto her desk. "My dad called. Apparently, a family friend died, and their memorial service is tomorrow."

At her announcement, I pushed the thought of seeing my brother aside for the moment and got up to hug my friend. "Oh no, Shawna, I'm so sorry."

Shawna shrugged under me. "Thank you, it's ok though. I didn't really know her. But you'll have the room to yourself tomorrow."

"Do you want me to go with you?" Even though she said it was ok, I knew losing someone was never easy.

"No, it's ok."

I squeezed her one more time then let her go. "If you want to talk about it, I'm here." She nodded and gave me a small smile that didn't reach her eyes.

I climbed back up to my bed and she stayed up to finish up some of her homework. I laid there for a long time, trying to go to sleep but nerves and excitement warred within me. On one hand I was nervous to go back out into the world in case I was attacked again. On the other hand, I was excited because I somehow summoned my brother. Kaden had said once that Owen had never been able to summon the dead. Tonight had to be because Owen and I were both Death and had a connection. I wanted to do it again, and I would practice every day until I could bring him back, even if it was only in ghost form.

The next morning, Shawna left early, dressed in black and looking somber. I offered to go with her again, but she politely declined. My heart went out to her and her family. I wondered if her parents left Italy and would be at the memorial today.

I stared around my room, wondering what to do now. It was so quiet without my roommate. I blasted some music and cleaned the room, then worked on my projects and homework. Tinkering with machinery helped calm my mind but I could not do it for long. My hand felt better than yesterday but it still stung when I used it too much which made tinkering difficult.

Giving up on it for now, I sat back and looked at the time on my phone. I groaned. It wasn't even lunch yet. Why did time go so slow when I was alone? I didn't have to be alone though. I could go train with Kaden. I tossed that idea aside. I wasn't ready to face them. I could go to the store to pick up some things Shawna and I needed. However, that meant going out into the world and I wasn't ready for that. Well, there was someone else I could talk to.

Spinning around in my desk chair I called out for my brother. "Owen!"

I felt silly calling for someone who wasn't there, but I was determined to see him again. Whether it was today, tomorrow, or a week from now.

"Owen, please show yourself." I waited but my brother did not appear. Deflating in disappointment I looked around the room for something else to do.

My eyes caught on the Religious Studies book on Shawna's desk. I could research the Horsemen some more. Maybe she had books that would give more details. I got up and flipped through her Religion Studies textbook, but it didn't hold anything about the Horsemen. Maybe I could read the Bible again to see if I missed anything. I knew her Bible was in one of the drawers of her desk, so I opened one looking for it. Thankfully it was in the same drawer I saw her take it out of last time. I picked it up and started to close the drawer again but a symbol on a piece of paper caught my eye. I placed the

Bible on the desk beside the textbook and picked up the paper from the drawer. My heart beat faster and dread settled in my stomach like a stone. It was a letter but at the top was a crest of a sword overlapping a cross on a blue and white four quadrant background.

No. no. no. no.

Dear Shawna Matthews,

You have been accepted into the Order of the Templars located at Penn State University. Our Order has thousands of members worldwide. You will be making a difference to better our world and continue to protect the innocent. We look forward to working with you.

I stopped reading, refusing to believe my roommate was one of…them. My heart pounded in my chest and panic made it impossible to breathe correctly. I needed to tell Liam and the others immediately. I grabbed my phone from my desk and tried to pull up Liam's name in my contacts. My hand shook making it difficult to do anything on the screen. I couldn't hold it straight enough to call or text. My other hand clutched the letter so tightly it was starting to crinkle. I stalked over to my roommate's desk and threw the letter back inside the drawer then grabbed my backpack. I was halfway out of the door when I paused and thought about what I was about to do.

If the others found out my roommate was a Templar and had been around me this whole time, they might kill her. As far as I knew she hadn't done anything to hurt me and she had plenty of chances. I shivered thinking about all the nights I slept soundly in my bed while Shawna was across the room. She could have killed me where I slept. Memories of the theater came to mind and I gasped. Did she tell them where I would be? No, she wouldn't have. Then again, she was a Templar, loyal only to the Order. Oh my God, was Shawna at that Templar's funeral right now? It was too much of a coincidence otherwise.

My head spun as I thought of all the moments Shawna and I had been together. Had she been faking our friendship? Pain spiked in my chest, but I pushed it away. This was no time to feel anything but wrath. I was going to get answers out of her as soon as she got back, and I would make sure she felt helpless and afraid just as I had felt whenever Templars were around.

I walked to my desk and rifled through my backpack until I found what I wanted. I set it out on my desk and grabbed a few other necessary supplies. Once I was sure I was ready, I sat down and waited.

Chapter 12

I heard a key jiggle the handle as the owner unlocked the door. I quickly grabbed the rag on my desk and stood behind the door. I had waited all afternoon. All the snacks in our room were gone because I didn't want to leave to get lunch. I had ignored a few texts from Kaden and Trevor. I did answer one from Liam after he asked about my hand and shoulder. I told him they were fine and left it at that. The rest of the day I tried to do homework or read but my mind constantly drifted to Shawna and her betrayal. Well, I was about to get answers.

The door opened and Shawna came in looking weary. I didn't give her time to react. I shoved the door closed with my foot and leapt on her back, bringing the rag with chloroform on it to her mouth and nose. Her shriek was muffled, and she threw us around the room attempting to toss me off. My back hurt after being knocked against walls and our desks, but I held on strong. Soon her struggles lessened, and she slumped. I caught her before she hit the floor and pushed her into her desk chair. Lacking rope, I used our bed sheets to tie her hands and feet to the chair and added some duct tape to her mouth. I made sure her nose was not blocked so she could still breathe then sat back in my desk chair to wait for her to wake.

My hands shook and blood pounded in my ears. I just attacked my roommate. Oh my God. I could be expelled for that. Probably locked up in an institution for that. Then the image of the cross with a sword in front came to mind and I narrowed my eyes at Shawna. She was the enemy. A trusted friend who had lied to me. I gripped my chair arms in anger.

"Owen!" I shouted, not caring if anyone outside heard.

I was upset with him too. Everything was fine until he said only to trust the Horsemen. I hated that he was right. I wanted to trust in someone else, but it seemed no one in my life was who they said they were.

A light appeared in front of me, momentarily blocking my line of sight to Shawna. Anticipation thrummed through me and I stood up with a smile. I may be upset that he was right, but I would always be happy to see him. A moment later, Owen's lighted, almost translucent, form appeared grinning at me.

"I knew you could do it. What were you feeling right before you called out to me?" he asked, unaware of the Templar tied up behind him.

I blinked at him, thrown off by the question. I tilted my head trying to remember what was different than earlier when I tried to call him. Images of his earnest expression telling me not to trust anyone then Shawna's betrayal made my chest ache.

"Anger, despair, and…" My eyes widened at the sudden realization that I had also been afraid. "and even a little bit of fear if I am being honest."

Owen grinned as if he had all the answers. I frowned waiting for him to enlighten me, but he stayed quiet.

When he still did not say anything I whined, "Owen, just tell me."

"The emotions you felt are the other Horsemen talents. It makes sense since death brings about all those emotions."

My mouth dropped open. It was so obvious now. If he was right, then I now knew how to summon Owen anytime I wanted and why it didn't work this morning. I was too excited and happy earlier but now my body shook with negative emotions. I would never be alone in this again. I finally succeeded at one thing as a Horseman. I squealed and jumped forward to hug him, but my body glided through and nearly fell upon Shawna's unconscious form.

I caught myself just before I landed on top of her and danced to the side. Owen turned, laughing at my lack of grace but frowned when he saw my roommate. His brow arched.

"Uh, care to tell me what this is about?"

My cheeks reddened and I crossed my arms, digging my nails into my skin before I did something I would regret. Like cause her to break out into black boils. Even though I was angry with Shawna and hurt that she would lie to me I still did not want her to die.

"She is a Templar."

I expected Owen to yell or tense, or even frown, but he only sighed. "That's it? You're not more upset by this?" I asked incredulously.

"I'm just not surprised by anything anymore. Well except the fact that I am talking to you right now." Owen shook his head and looked away.

For the first time I wondered how all the Horsemen stuff affected him when he was alive. He said he got into fights because of it but there had to be more. My heart ached for him and what he must have gone through. He learned he could not trust anyone. Sadly, I was coming to the same conclusion. It all made for a lonely existence.

Shawna groaned and suddenly I was on the other side of the room, as far from her as I could get. I had been in the same room as her for months now, but now that I knew who she was, I was terrified. I knew she was tied to her chair and could not harm me, but I had been attacked twice now by Templars. I did not exactly want to face another one.

Owen glanced from her to me with amusement. "Aren't you going to interrogate her?"

I bit my lip and watched as my roommate came to and looked around. Her eyes skipped over Owen telling me she couldn't see him. Interesting. Maybe it was because she wasn't a Horseman. When her eyes landed on me, she frowned and yanked her arms as if she was going to lunge at me. She did not get far due to the sheets keeping her arms secured. She glanced at her arms and legs then back at me with a new expression. It almost looked like fear. That couldn't be right though. She was a Templar. They only knew hate and pride.

Owen nodded his head toward her, urging me to get closer and demand answers. I glanced from him to Shawna then clenched my fists in determination. I was a freaking Horseman. Death to be precise. I should not be cowering in a corner.

I walked over until I was standing in front of her then ripped the duct tape off forcefully causing her to wince. I wanted to shout at her and rage about how she had lied to me but when I saw how helpless she looked and frightened though she tried to hide it behind a glare, my anger slipped away.

Instead, one word slipped out, and the way my voice cracked made it sound pathetic. "Why?"

Shawna growled, or tried to but it caught in her throat and she ended up coughing. My brows rose in surprise at her lack of intimidation. She was definitely not like the other two Templars I came across. I almost wanted to laugh but I knew that would only make her mood worse.

Owen had no qualms about it. Good thing Shawna couldn't see or hear him because he filled the room with his laughter. I shot him a look to shut up then focused on Shawna again.

Getting herself back under control, she glowered and grit her teeth as she said, "Why am I tied up, Ophelia?"

Ouch. She called me Ophelia, which she knew I hated. It also meant she considered me a stranger now. Well, she was a stranger to me, so it was fair.

"How could you betray me like that?" I asked, surprised by the slight hissing in my tone.

Shawna's eyes rounded briefly before she forced her expression to be one of confusion. "I don't know what you're talking about."

I looked at Owen and threw my hands up in exasperation. Owen shook his head. "Just tell her everything you know so she can stop this pathetic innocent act. If I were corporeal, I would have punched her already."

I rolled my eyes at my brother's violent thoughts and grabbed the crumpled letter I found in Shawna's desk. I held it out in front of her and watched her reaction. Shawna's eyes roamed over it and widened, finally looking at me with a new fear.

"You are part of the Templar Order. An Order which has been hunting me and my friends."

Shawna opened her mouth to say something, but I kept going.

"An Order that almost killed me yesterday."

Shawna looked shocked but tried to speak again. My voice rose to cut off whatever she was going to say.

"An Order that killed my brother!"

At that, Shawna's mouth snapped shut and her scrunched brows told me she had no idea about that.

I felt anger toward her and the Templars. Even though she probably had not been the one to kill Owen, I felt that loss all over again and blamed her. My chest ached with sadness, anger, and fear that it might happen again. I heard Owen calling my name, but it was distant. Without thinking I reached out and touched Shawna's cheek, wanting her to feel what I felt.

Shawna cried out and tried to roll into a ball, but the restraints prevented her. Tears cascaded down her face and she pleaded in whispers for me to stop. I pushed harder, pouring everything out of me and into her. I wanted her to know what her Order had done to me and Owen.

"Phi!"

My mind snapped out of the grief-stricken haze at Owen's voice. I realized what I was doing and pulled back from Shawna in horror.

Oh no, what have I done?

I checked over my roommate looking for black patches or boils. When I found none, I sighed in relief. Owen's wide eyes met mine and after a moment he smiled. Any other time I would have found that weird, but

I was sure I had a matching one. Our smiles probably made it look like I enjoyed inflicting that pain, but we were smiling about something else. I had successfully used my talent without killing someone. I think it had to do with the fact that it was a different kind of sickness I felt and extended to her. A sickness caused by grief rather than a virus. It would be interesting to try out my new idea in training but for now I had a Templar to deal with.

Shawna breathed heavily and looked up to me, her eyes still red and tear tracks stained her cheeks, but she was no longer crying. "I never knew," Shawna whispered, her voice cracking.

Now that I had expunged some of my feelings and made her feel what I felt all the time, I was calmer. Still mad and hurt but calm.

After a few minutes of quiet, Shawna whispered again. "I never had a choice."

I scowled at her but couldn't help but ask. "What do you mean?" I probably should have left by now and never come back to that room, but I wanted answers. My mind argued that fact though since she was a Templar, but I felt if Shawna wanted to, she could have harmed me anytime within the past few weeks so a couple more minutes wouldn't hurt.

"I am a legacy. I never had a choice to join the Templars." She sounded sad yet resigned.

I looked to Owen, "Legacy?" I asked him, wondering if he knew about legacies within the Templar Order.

He shook his head and shrugged. Shawna followed my line of sight and frowned, not seeing Owen and probably thinking I was as crazy as the Templars probably made me out to be.

"What's a legacy?" I asked, covering up the fact I had been talking to the air.

"It's someone who was born into the Order. Both of my parents are important Templars."

Oh snap, so when she said her parents were schmoozing with the Pope, she was serious. Shawna had said her dad traveled a lot. He was probably a leader of the Templars or something similar. I was suddenly glad I had not met her parents. They were probably the kill-first-ask-questions-later type.

"Why haven't you killed me yet?" I asked. If she was a legacy and had grown up around all that Templar crap, then her first priority would be to kill me and the others.

Shawna scrunched up her nose. "I never believed in the Horsemen. My parents did not talk about them much since they traveled a lot. The Order is much more than just hunting down some fictional people anyway." She looked at me hesitantly. "However, now I know the Templars were right." She didn't give me a chance to respond. She was probably trying to explain herself quickly before I left or hurt her again. "I was put in here as your roommate because it was suspected you were a Horseman. However, I didn't believe it. I never told them anything about you or the others."

I bit my lip thinking about what she said. I glanced at Owen to see what he made of it, but he disappeared. I turned around looking for him, but he was gone. We really had to figure out how the whole ghost thing worked. I focused back on Shawna, thinking about yesterday.

"Did you tell that Templar girl where we would be yesterday?" I attempted to keep my face nonchalant, but my blood simmered underneath. No matter her words, I had been attacked by her people and that was something I would not forget.

"Templar girl? What do you- Oh my God. That's how she died? You killed her?" Disbelief and fear tinged her words then her eyes widened, and she looked over my body with worry. "Is she the reason you came home all cut up?"

I couldn't tell if she was angry with me or concerned. I nodded slowly, not saying a word.

"Then she got what she deserved," Shawna said, holding her chin up defiantly.

My brows drew down at her words. She was okay with her fellow Templar dying yet she feared me a moment before when she figured out I killed her. All of this was causing me to be paranoid and confused. I needed to leave and clear my head. I moved away from her, toward my side of the room to grab my backpack but Shawna made me pause when she spoke again.

"Phi, I don't believe you are an evil person. I know you. You would never intentionally hurt someone unless they hurt you first. I will not tell them about you. You can trust me."

I kept my back to her thinking over what she said. She was right. I would never intentionally hurt someone unless they were hurting me or someone I loved. But, could I trust her? My head said no, but my heart tried saying something else. I was too confused and hurt right now. I grabbed my bag and threw some clothes into it.

"Where are you going?" Shawna asked softly.

"I don't know but I can't stay here." I knew where I would go but there was no way I would alert her to my plans or whereabouts.

I paused right before I left and contemplated what I should do with Shawna. She was a Templar so I should leave her here tied up so she couldn't alert her Order, but she seemed so innocent. Not once had she tried to hurt me or the others. The only thing she had done wrong was lie.

Before I could change my mind, I grabbed a pair of scissors and put them into her hand then walked out, leaving her alone. By the time she freed herself with the scissors I would be long gone.

Now I had to explain to the guys why I suddenly decided to stay at their place.

Chapter 13

I didn't bother knocking. I walked in and threw my stuff on the kitchen table and rifled through their fridge. I must have made some noise because a moment later, three pairs of footsteps thundered down the stairs.

"Phi? What are you doing here?" Trevor asked when they all came into the kitchen to find me pouring lemonade into a glass.

Seeing them with looks of concern almost broke me. I turned away and took a deep breath to hold in my tears. When I turned back towards them, it was with a smile and glass of lemonade.

"I ran out of lemonade," I told them, then moved to sit at the table.

They followed me, taking seats as well, and stared. I sipped my drink slowly, avoiding their eyes and hoping they couldn't read on my face that something was wrong. I must have failed because Liam grunted and asked, "Did something happen? Tell us," then grabbed my injured hand, turning it over to check the wound.

I pulled my hand back and set my glass on the table before fiddling with my bracelet. Now was the time to tell them about Shawna. They needed to know yet something held me back. I felt protective of my roommate despite her deceit. I remembered yesterday how Trevor admitted they had killed before and didn't regret it. I knew if the guys found out about her they would act and by tomorrow, Shawna might be the next missing person. I couldn't do that to her, so we would call it even. She didn't tell the Templars about us so I wouldn't tell the Horsemen about her.

"Phi," Kaden said softly, reminding me I needed to say something.

I couldn't just tell them I felt like being around them or I felt unsafe because that would bring about more unwanted questions. They were already alert since it was not normal for me to arrive unannounced especially with a packed bag. I sighed.

"Phi," Liam said in a low voice.

Where Kaden sounded concerned, Liam sounded almost threatening. I glared at him, letting him know he couldn't boss me around. Then I thought of the perfect thing to tell them.

"So, I kinda, sorta summoned Owen as a ghost."

They stared at me with wide eyes. Trevor's mouth hung open and Kaden glanced from me to Liam wondering if I was joking. Then they all started speaking at once, the volume in the room going up by the second. I held out my hands to stop the voices and they shut up to let me explain.

"It was yesterday at home and again this morning. I called out to him and he appeared. I think I can do it because we are both Death." I looked at all of them wondering what they thought. It could not be the craziest thing they have heard of.

"You really saw him?" Trevor asked letting out a breath.

"And talked to him?" Kaden added, eyes wide and mouth hanging open.

I nodded, my eyes landing on Liam. He didn't say anything, just stared at me. I could not pick up what he was thinking or feeling. It made me a bit uncomfortable. I shifted in my seat and looked away.

"That's amazing!" Kaden shouted, causing me to flinch at the sound. "I've gotta research this." Kaden got up and walked upstairs muttering under his breath excitedly.

Research? This whole time I had been poking through the Bible, yet Kaden had actual research materials. I made a mental note to bug him about using them later.

"What did he say?" Trevor asked, clasping his hands in front of him on the table and leaning forward expectantly.

"We just talked about Horsemen stuff, like how all the people you beat up in High School were Templars."

"Except Johnny Marks," Trevor said chuckling.

"Freaking Johnny Marks," Liam said, crossing his arms, and a small smile played at his lips.

My own lips pulled into a smile at their behavior. They sounded just like Owen. I told them more about seeing Owen and what it was like and what we figured out about my talents. I left out any mention of Shawna, but they did not seem to notice. Eventually, my yawn interrupted our conversation and Trevor called it a night.

"See you in the morning," Trevor said to us before climbing the stairs to his room.

I shifted in my seat when Liam and I were alone. He stared at me, but I couldn't tell what was going through his head. His brows drew down a bit and he looked at me thoughtfully. Wanting to escape the intense stare I got up and put my glass in the sink.

"I should probably go to bed too." I moved toward the stairs and got up a few before footsteps followed me.

I intended to ignore the heat from Liam behind me, but it became impossible when he grabbed me and gently pushed me against the wall, trapping me with his body. My heart beat faster and I stared up at him with wide eyes.

"Liam? What-"

"Are you ok, Phi?"

His question shocked me into silence. How did he know something was wrong? I had covered up my roiling emotions so well, or so I thought.

"I-I'm fine," I said, my voice catching a little. I chalked it up to a lump in my throat and not the nervousness I felt with him standing so close.

He stepped in a little further and I pressed as far into the wall as I could, not wanting him to see how my body seemed to be affected by his hard muscles and heat. I growled and pushed against his chest, wanting some space to clear my head. I was not going to be one of those girls I had seen around him falling into a puddle just at his proximity.

He gave me a crooked smile at my attempt and caught my hand in one of his. Which only made my heart race faster. Stupid hormones.

"Something else happened today didn't it?" He asked softly, leaning in.

My breath caught and I looked anywhere but his eyes. His eyes were hypnotizing, and I knew if I looked into them, I might blurt everything out. "What makes you say that?" Yes! My voice sounded strong that time. I was totally not affected by him.

His eyes narrowed bringing my focus back to them. "Phi," he warned.

Suddenly, I was back to myself. Funny how saying my name like I was about to be in trouble if I didn't comply would do that. "Liam," I said back.

"You know what I can do," he said with a smirk.

My mouth gaped open. So that's how he wanted this to go. He thought he could use his charm to make me spill my secrets and if that didn't work then he would resort to his talent for fear?

I laughed in his face. "Nice try."

I sidled out from between him and the wall and raced up the stairs not giving him a chance to act on his warning.

I thought he would follow but I only heard his chuckle before I closed myself in the guest bedroom. I didn't move away from the door until my heartbeat slowed then I shook my head, annoyed with him. Man, he was so manipulative. I couldn't let him get that close again. I almost blurted out Shawna's secret and that would have been catastrophic. Seriously though, what was his deal? I needed to talk to Owen about him sometime. Kaden and Trevor were easy to be around, but I was always on guard around Liam, wondering how he would react to every little thing. He seemed to be caring once second then he acted as if I should tell him everything because I would regret it otherwise.

He never used to be like that. I actually got along quite well with them all before Owen died. I was one of the only people who could walk up to them and not get punched and get a genuine smile out of them. Ever since I started hanging with them again, Trevor and Kaden had fallen back into our old companionship, but Liam had been on edge whenever he was around me even though he tried to hide it underneath his smirks and superiority complex. I grumbled and decided to put it all out of my mind. I really did not need to be worrying about Liam on top of everything else.

A few days went by and I still refused to go to my dorm unless Shawna was not there. I knew Shawna's schedule so I made sure to stop by for extra clothes or necessities when she would not be there. Otherwise I was in class or at the house with the guys. Liam never tried to ask me what was wrong again, but I found him watching me when he thought no one noticed.

I was in the guest bedroom, tinkering with a machine for my Engineering class, when my phone gave out a loud siren noise, like those sounds phones get when there is an emergency message. I dove to turn the sound off and could hear other phones in the house making the same noise. I had just pressed okay on my phone to silence the noise so I could read the message when footsteps thundered down the hall and three sets of bodies came crashing into my room, holding up their phones and looking worried.

"What? What's wrong?" I asked hurriedly, my thoughts going to Shawna and my parents. I may be still upset with Shawna, but I didn't want to see her dead.

"Did you kill more people?" Trevor asked.

I stared at them with a slack jaw and wide eyes. Then outrage took over. "What? Of course not!"

"Then what is this?" Kaden asked holding his phone out to me.

I took it and saw the emergency message that I hadn't had a chance to read on my phone. I murmured to myself as I read then gasped. "Outbreak of a mysterious virus on campus? Three dead? When did this happen?" I asked looking up at them expectantly.

"Today, apparently. And you're sure that wasn't you?" Kaden asked.

I bristled and threw his phone at him. He flinched but caught it midair then patted his phone checking to see if I broke it. "Of course I didn't do this!"

Liam frowned at his friends then stepped forward to get my attention. "I believe you. But it means the Templars will be pointing fingers at you anyway and you will be in even more danger."

I looked at him relieved to know someone believed me then his other words penetrated my mind. I threw my hands in the air in exasperation. "Of course they will."

I sighed with resignation. There was nothing we could do except lay low and keep an eye on how it progressed.

 If it progressed.

And it did progress. Over the next week five more people came down with the mysterious illness, all students from Penn State. A new warning was issued to take precautions and wash our hands and to keep our distance from others. School was still in session but now I was even more worried about being hunted by Templars. There were eight dead now and anyone who knew the Horsemen were real would be pointing to me as the culprit. Maybe I did cause it and I just didn't realize. I shook my head at the thought. I would have known if I used my power to create an epidemic.

Right?

I was at the kitchen table doing homework when there was a knock on the door. Kaden and Trevor were in the living room watching TV, and they glanced to the door. I tilted my head at it telling them to answer it and went back to my homework. I needed to focus on school rather than an epidemic that I may or may not have caused. Kaden grumbled something about pausing the show so he wouldn't miss anything before going to the door to see who was there. A friendly and slightly flirty voice reached me making me tense. Kaden stood in front of her chatting and flirting right back not knowing that a Templar stood in his presence. I felt instantly protective of him and my ex-roommate and rushed to the door, sliding in between him and Shawna.

To anyone else, she would look like her normal, stylish self with dark blue skinny jeans, pink camisole, and impeccable makeup on her soft mocha skin. However, I knew her better and I could see that her smile didn't reach her eyes and that there was hesitance and sadness within their brown depths.

"Whoa, careful, you almost stepped on my feet," Kaden joked and put his hands on my shoulders to steady us.

I ignored him and crossed my arms in front of my chest glaring at my roommate. "What do you want?" I asked, my voice cold and uncaring.

Kaden continued smiling but his hands tightened on my shoulders, the only indication he picked up on our tense encounter. I knew Liam would hear about this from Kaden, but I would deal with that later.

She kept the smile on her face, but it fell slightly. Shawna glanced at Kaden hesitantly then looked at me with pleading eyes. "I was hoping we could talk."

"There isn't anything to talk about." I grabbed the edge of the door and started to close it in her face, but she held out a perfectly manicured hand to stop it. I glared at the hand willing it to disappear, but it stayed. She dropped her smile and frowned. "Phi, talk to me. I have something you might want to know."

I was curious I would admit that, but I definitely did not want to talk while Kaden was standing there. Deciding to hear her out just for a minute, I sighed and stepped out of the house to indulge her. I turned my head to Kaden, raising my brow as if to say he could leave now.

He glanced from Shawna to me and nodded slowly, confusion in his expression. He closed the door and I led her to the side of the house in case Kaden was standing near the door eavesdropping. I didn't think Horsemen had super hearing but better safe than sorry.

"I'm surprised to see you here. How did you find me?" I asked.

She gave me a look like I was an idiot for asking. "Where else would you go?"

True. "Why are you here? What if Kaden attacked you?" I didn't mean to sound concerned but it slipped out.

A slow grin spread over her face and I rolled my eyes, not wanting to let her know I cared. "I had to take a chance. I figured they didn't know or else they would have hunted me down already." Then she frowned and tilted her head. "Right? From the way you have spoken of them I assume that's what they would have done."

I frowned and looked at the side of the house grumbling. Her grin spread and suddenly she sprung forward and hugged me. I tensed, a shout lodged in my throat. The shout turned to a lump and tears pricked my eyes. I hadn't realized how much I wanted to see her again as a friend and not a potential enemy until right then. I shook my feelings away and pushed her back.

"That doesn't mean we are friends."

Hurt flashed in her eyes before she masked it. She nodded and cleared her throat. "Right. But, Phi" I looked up when she paused. "I will not hurt you or them." She seemed to hesitate a moment before she straightened her back and looked at me with a determined tilt to her chin. "And I know you didn't cause the outbreak."

I searched her face to see if she was telling the truth. I was stunned she trusted me enough to know I wouldn't hurt people with my Horseman power, even after eight people died from a mysterious illness. I knew Owen said not to trust anyone and he ended up being right, but I perceived no deception from her. I would not be able to trust her completely for a while but at least I could accept her statement and be glad at least one person out there believed in me.

"Is that what you came to say?"

"No, well yes, but not just that."

I quirked a brow waiting for her to continue. She started murmuring to herself and fiddling with her hands. This was new. I had never seen her so nervous. I picked up the words trouble and Order from her murmuring, but I couldn't make sense of it.

"Shawna," I urged, reminding her she still had not said anything.

Shawna's eyes widened and she looked around before bringing her focus back to me. "At the last meeting, the Order talked about bringing in some professionals."

I frowned, and my chest tightened with dread. That sounded bad. "Professionals? What do you mean?"

Shawna huffed in exasperation. "Professionals, like the Inquisition but for hunting Horsemen. You know? They want to get rid of you before any more people fall sick and die."

My eyes widened at her announcement. "What, why do they think it was me?" I suspected the Templars blamed the outbreak on me, but I didn't think they would bring in professional killers. "Outbreaks happen on their own all the time." My voice rose to almost screechy proportions and I cleared my throat to reset it to its normal tone.

Shawna nodded but her expression told me she was going to impart bad news. "Yes, but the evidence is against you."

I shook my head. "Pshh, what evidence?"

Shawna started ticking off things on her fingers. "One, the Death Horseman is in town. Two, it's a mysterious illness that no one can figure out how it spreads or started. Three, every victim had a small mark almost like a scythe on their forearm."

I blinked at number three. "Wait, what? A mark? I don't leave any scythe marks when I use pestilence."

Shawna nodded like she already suspected that. "And now professionals have been summoned to take you out before it gets worse."

I shook my head trying to dislodge the information she just gave me, but it only dug itself deeper into my mind. "Oh no, this isn't good. I've gotta tell them right now." I moved toward the front of the house, but Shawna gripped my arm stopping me.

"They will be here within the next two weeks, that's all I know. They don't usually tell us anything but since they will be on campus, we were told to be aware of their presence and help them get around." She stared at me with worry and fear.

That scared me more than anything. If a Templar feared these hunters then we should too. Great, I just couldn't catch a break. I touched her hand that was still gripping my arm. "Thank you for telling me." I started to walk away but turned back, hesitating a moment before asking, "could you keep me updated?"

She nodded emphatically. "Be careful, Phi." Then she walked away leaving me to think over her words. I had a class in a little bit but there was no way I would feel comfortable going now, despite Shawna saying the hunters wouldn't be there for a couple weeks.

I breathed in and out deeply to calm myself. I couldn't barge into the house telling them about this new threat. They would question where I got the information from. Kaden would remember the way I acted around Shawna and they would figure it all out. No, I couldn't do that to her. She risked herself to get me that information.

We needed to prepare and find some way to get rid of these professionals. I would figure out a story then tell the guys. I walked into the house, schooling my expression and went back to the kitchen table where my homework was laid out. I felt Trevor and Kaden's questioning eyes on me, but I ignored them. I would have to fake being sick in a bit so I could get out of going to class with minimal questions being tossed my way.

I went back to completing my homework but jumped when a hand landed on the textbook I was reading. I hadn't heard anyone approach. I looked at the hand and followed it up the arm to broad shoulders and a smiling Liam looking down at me. I rolled my eyes and pushed his hand off, going back to my homework. He put his hand back on the book and I sat back, huffing at him.

"What do you want?"

His smile grew. "Let's go for a ride."

"Excuse me?"

He rolled his eyes and stood up straight, crossing his arms. "You know what I mean."

I narrowed my eyes. What was his angle? "Where to?"

"A place," he answered and gave me look daring me to ask about it.

I knew if I asked what place he would give me another vague answer. At least this was a good way to get out of going to class. However, going anywhere mysterious with Liam sounded like a bad idea. Instead of accepting or asking where we were going, I turned away and drew my textbook to me. "No thanks."

Liam sighed and snagged my book, making me protest. "C'mon, trust me. You'll like it."

I eyed him suspiciously, but he didn't seem to be tricking me. I glanced around him to see if Kaden and Trevor knew where we were going but they only looked at us curiously, which told me they didn't know. I looked back at Liam and raised my eyebrow. I was curious about where he wanted to take me, but it was Liam. Who knew what his actual plans were? He probably wanted to torture some poor kids by making me practice my talent or to interrogate me about Shawna and our odd behavior. Either way I wouldn't fall for it.

"Just tell me where we are going," I tried.

He sighed in exasperation and grabbed my arm pulling me up from the chair. "Why do you have to be so difficult? It's just a ride."

I shot a look to Kaden and Trevor mouthing help me as we passed them on the way to the door. They only chuckled and went back to their TV show. Liam led me outside, his hand still on my arm in case I ran away. There is a high possibility I would have done just that. He didn't let go until we were in front of his white motorcycle where he handed me a helmet.

"Get on," he ordered after settling himself on it first.

I threw my head back and sighed loudly before getting on the back as he instructed. "Fine. But don't think you can order me around all day."

I thought I saw him smile but he turned away before I could be sure. "Hold on tight."

Another order, but I let it slide since the engine's roar would drown out any protests. Despite my wariness of his destination and the new threat hiding somewhere out there I squealed in delight as we zoomed away with the air flowing through my hair and speed making my heart race with adrenaline.

Chapter 14

I lost track of where we were by the fourth turn and eventually, we were on a highway. I settled against Liam and let the noise and breeze wash over me. Riding on a motorcycle made me feel free of worries. Like I could go anywhere and do anything. Riding on a motorcycle was one of my favorite things, even though I had lost it when Owen died. If there was one thing I loved about becoming a Horseman it was finding my love of motorcycles again. Well, that and the fact that I could talk to my brother again.

I must have closed my eyes at some point because the next thing I knew, we were slowing down. My eyes popped open and took in our surroundings. I had no idea how long we were driving but we somehow ended up in a largely forested area and I swore I could smell water. Well, I could smell the air that a large body of water creates. I didn't know how to explain it, but I smelt it and felt excited at the possibility of going to a lake. I knew it was not the ocean because Penn State was nowhere near the ocean so lake was the only thing it could be.

I took my helmet off when we stopped and handed it over to Liam. He grinned at me mischievously and grabbed my hand, leading me down a hiking trail near the bike. I waited a few minutes but when he continued the silence my impatience grew. "Where are we?"

"In a forest," he replied without turning around. He continued holding my hand even though I had eyes and could have followed him fine without the guiding hand.

I rolled my eyes even though he couldn't see and tried again. "Yes, but where are we going?"

"You'll see."

I frowned and decided to do to him what he once did to me. I focused on the feeling of loss and sickness that death causes and shot it out of my hand that Liam held. I knew it worked when he jerked to a stop and started breathing deeply. He bent over a little to contain the feeling of sickness but a second later I yelped and pulled my hand away when a shot of fear entered my system.

He stood up straight, the sick feeling having left his body, and chuckled. "You don't want to mess with me."

We would see about that. I decided I was more curious about our destination, so I kept my talents to myself for now, though I promised myself I would get him later. We came across a bridge and I stopped. It looked rickety and the drop may not kill me if I were to fall but it would definitely hurt. I was not a big fan of heights. Well, actually I was fine with heights but not falling and that bridge looked like it would give way any moment.

"Tell me we are not crossing that."

Liam walked onto it and looked back at me, giving me a smile that dared me to get closer. I inched closer until I met him a few feet on the bridge then looked down. It was a small drop, about fifteen feet down but far enough that I didn't want to fall. I started to back up to solid ground, but Liam reached out and grabbed my hand, pulling me toward him. I expected him to move but he stayed still, and I ended up crashing against his chest. I felt his heart beating fast and looked up into his eyes to see something I wasn't ready to acknowledge. I pulled back but he maneuvered us until he was behind me and I had nowhere else to go but forward to the other side.

Liam brought his lips near my ear and whispered, "Trust me," causing shivers to race down my neck and arms.

I moved forward to avoid the heat his body radiated and tried to calm my emotions. This was no time to be developing a crush. A little voice in my head tried saying the crush had already been there but I squashed it down. I gripped the ropes on either side of me and slowly made my way across. Somehow, I made it and breathed a sigh of relief when my feet landed on solid ground again. Liam came up beside me a second later and took charge again, leading us farther. This time we didn't have to walk far, and I jumped in delight when I saw water.

"I knew it!" I shouted punching the air in victory.

Liam raised an eyebrow at my delight, but I knew it amused him if the small smile was any indication. "No, you didn't."

"Yes, I did, I totally smelled it." I raised my chin in defiance and put my hands on my hips.

"You…smelled it?" He shook his head and chuckled as he pushed my shoulder playfully. "You're a dork."

I scoffed but couldn't stop my own smile. I enjoyed seeing Liam open and happy, but I was a little tense waiting for his mood to change and ruin the moment. At least I could enjoy the light heartedness while it lasted. We walked over to the rocks by the water and I got a good look at our surroundings. It was too small to be a lake but too big to be a pond. I had no idea what it was, but the water was clear and there were boulders nearby that acted as barriers. Liam stripped off his shirt and my breath caught.

"Uh, what're you doing?"

My eyes roamed over his chest and arms, taking in all the muscles and tattoos he had. There was one of a bow and arrow on his left bicep which I knew was his Horseman symbol. On his left side, along his ribs under his arm, in descending order were the other Horseman symbols: sword, scales, and scythe. He turned to put his shirt on a nearby rock and I saw a date with a cross on his right shoulder blade. It was the date Owen died. I wanted to step closer and run my fingers over the marks on his skin. To trace the lines of his muscles and feel his warmth.

"We are going to swim," he said turning back to me with a frown like it was obvious.

I blinked, remembering I had asked him a question and forced my eyes to meet his rather than looking at his bare chest. "We?"

"Yes, we." His hands went to his pants and he started unbuttoning them.

I squeaked and turned around. "Um, no, I'm good. I don't really want to go swimming." That was a lie. I loved swimming. However, there was no way I was going to take my clothes off and swim around with a mostly naked Liam.

"Suit yourself." I heard a splash and turned around to see the surface of the water disturbed. A second later, Liam popped up from underwater and grinned at me. "The water is nice, you're missing out."

I crept closer and peered into the water. I couldn't see his body, the water just dark enough to cover him but I still refused. I sat next to his clothes and noticed only his shirt, pants, and shoes were on the rock, meaning he had kept his underwear on. Good.

For a second, I thought about grabbing his clothes and making a run for it, but I discarded that idea. No need to cause trouble. Yet.

I took my shoes and socks off, then drew my knees up and hugged them while looking around at the beautiful surroundings. How had he found that place? The water was hidden by the trees and in order to get to it, one had to drive to who knew where and cross a suspicious looking bridge. I closed my eyes and leaned my head back, taking a large inhale. The air was so fresh. I could spend hours there.

I opened my eyes and looked back to the water, looking for Liam to ask him about the place but he was nowhere to be seen. I dropped my knees and inched closer, looking for any disturbance in the water so I knew where he was at. My heart started racing in panic when I found no trace of him. Oh my God. Did he drown?

No. No. No. No

I jumped down from the rock and took a few steps into the water. "Liam!" I called out.

Silence reigned.

"Li- ah!"

He suddenly popped up in front of me from under the water and wrapped his arms around me. He pulled me into the water with him until I was fully submerged. He let go when I was completely soaked and I swam upward, breaking through to the surface and spluttering. He followed and laughed deeply at my appearance.

I glared at him, water dripping from my hair into my eyes. I dove for him and pushed him under, enacting my revenge. We wrestled in the water and splashed each other for a while, both of us laughing, until we were too tired to continue. We ended up floating in comfortable silence when our energy was spent.

"Thanks for bringing me here," I said, breaking the silence.

"This is my favorite place to go when I want to get away," he responded.

It warmed me inside that he chose to bring me here to be part of this place. Again, I wondered how he had come across it. I opened my mouth to ask but he spoke, halting my words.

"You've been through a lot lately."

I stayed quiet, not knowing how to respond. I felt it was rhetorical because of course I've been through a lot. My life had changed, and new surprises kept coming up refusing to let me settle into this new supernatural life.

"You were never meant to be a part of this," he added.

I bristled, offended that he still thought I couldn't handle it all, but immediately calmed when I noticed there was no venom in his words. He was just stating a fact, not trying to put me down. I thought about it a moment, trying to see it from his perspective. Owen had been the Horseman and I had been the oblivious twin. I should have gone to college none the wiser.

"Yeah, but I am now, and you know what? I am glad for it." Except the whole killing two people thing.

The water shifted as Liam faced me. I turned to see him better and flapped my arms and legs to keep myself afloat. He studied me, trying to determine whether I really was glad to be part of the Horsemen or if I was putting on a brave face. He must have been satisfied with what he saw because he smiled but then his smile dimmed, and he looked down at the water.

"I'm sorry, Phi."

"For what?" I knew there were tons of things he could apologize for such as drugging me, using his talent on me, dunking me in the water, or ordering me around, but something else seemed to be weighing on him and I couldn't fathom what it would be.

"I'm sorry I didn't save Owen. I'm sorry you were dragged into this."

Oh my goodness. Liam felt guilty over Owen's death. I never made him feel any better about it either. I felt guilt trickle inside me. Back when I did not know about the Horsemen or the Templars, I had blamed Liam and the others for encouraging Owen to ride motorcycles. When I learned the truth, I let go of that blame. It was not their fault that their friend, their pseudo brother, was murdered. Except I never did anything to let them know I didn't blame them anymore. I was a terrible friend.

I reached out and touched his cheek making him look back at me. "Liam, you have nothing to be sorry about."

He gently took my hand from his face and held it under the water. His eyes glistened and for a second and I thought he was going to cry. "Yes, I do. I was there the day he died. I couldn't save him. Now I am doing everything I can to save you from the same fate but you're too stubborn. Why can't you do as I say and stay safe? You mean too much to me."

My eyes widened at his declaration. I meant too much to him? What did he mean? Like a sister, or something more? I didn't want to dwell on it in case I misinterpreted his words. Instead I focused on what else he said. I squeezed his hand and bit my lips to force down a chuckle. He had been trying to push me away for weeks, but I kept coming back, challenging his authority and orders. While his actions had not been stellar, I now understood that he was scared and tried to prevent me from getting hurt.

"Liam, I am here to stay. Now that I am a Horseman, I would be in more danger on my own. And don't feel guilty about Owen, I know you did everything you could to help him." I put all my sincerity behind my words so he knew I did not blame him and that he should not carry around guilt any longer.

If Liam was there the day Owen died, then he would have fought with everything he had to save my twin. I did not doubt his ability and strength so while it was a shock to find out Liam was there, I felt more sympathy than anything because he had to witness my brother's end.

Liam tugged on my hand, forcing me to float towards him. I thought he was going in for a hug, but he brought his hand up and cupped my cheek then leaned down and brought his lips to mine. My eyes went wide, and I squeaked at the suddenness of it all, but then I felt his lips move and I melted against him. I closed my eyes and threw my free arm around his shoulders bringing our bodies closer even though I didn't think that was possible.

I had been kissed before, but nothing came close to being kissed by Liam Griffiths. Heat radiated from him despite being in the water and the stubble on his jaw scratched against my chin sending shivers down my body. I moaned against his mouth, enjoying the feelings cascading through me that he caused. I felt him smile and he bit my bottom lip before soothing it with another kiss.

"Oh, get a room already!"

I shrieked and pushed away from Liam, turning in the water to find the source of the voice.

"What's wrong?" Liam asked from my left, his posture alert.

Owen floated above the water with crossed arms, staring down at us with a jokingly disgusted look. "I'm gone for, like, two seconds and you're jumping my best friend. I object!"

"Wha- I'm- no," I stammered, looking up to see Owen's lips twitching as he fought a smile.

"What are you saying? What's going on?" Liam asked, getting closer and looking around to find what I was looking at.

I turned my head, keeping Owen in my peripherals, to look at Liam. His brows were furrowed in confusion as he studied our surroundings. I noticed his lips were a little red and swollen and smiled to myself, loving that I caused that.

"So, my brother is here judging us," I stated casually.

"Owen? He's here?" Liam spun in a circle in the water, looking for the ghostly form of my twin.

I chuckled and pointed to the air where Owen floated. Liam squinted at the spot but shook his head letting me know he couldn't see him. So maybe it was just a Death thing.

I focused on Owen again. "Why are you here? I didn't summon you."

"Well, you kind of did." At my confused look Owen explained, "his emotions," he pointed to Liam, "were the necessary bits to summon me then you both started saying my name and voila, I am here." He bowed as if he just performed a magic trick.

I relayed the explanation to Liam, and he nodded though I wasn't sure how much he actually understood.

I cleared my throat, remembering what I had been doing a minute ago. "So, uh, how much did you see?"

Owen's face morphed into disgust. "Too much."

My cheeks reddened and Liam chuckled, understanding his answer without having to hear him. "Well you can go now." I turned away and started swimming to shore. I was a little perturbed that Owen interrupted my kiss with Liam, but also thankful for it. I had no idea why Liam kissed me and while I enjoyed it, I felt it would make things complicated among the

Horsemen. My muscles ached from having to support myself in the water for so long, but I finally made it to shore.

Owen chuckled and appeared on the rock where Liam's clothes and my shoes were laid out. I reached him and pulled myself up onto the rock. Owen looked over everything then narrowed his eyes at me. "You were swimming with him and kissing him while he is only in his underwear?"

My cheeks reddened further at the reminder. I heard Liam get out of the water, so I kept my gaze averted. Owen moved his glare to Liam and started cursing at him and muttering things about seducing his sister and how he will haunt his ass if he does it again and other sorts of nonsense. I snorted but stayed quiet knowing I was the only one who could hear him.

"Could you hand me my clothes?" Liam said from behind me.

I grabbed them and held them behind my back, continuing to keep my eyes away from Liam's nearly naked body. Liam took them and I waited for him to get dressed.

"Ok, you can turn around now."

I did and my heart raced at seeing the jeans hang low on his hips and his chest bare since he did not put on a shirt yet. I moved closer, wanting to run my fingers over his chest but Owen floated down from the rock and stood in front of Liam, glaring at me with his arms crossed.

I rolled my eyes and sat down instead to tie my shoes.

"I hope that wasn't an eye roll at me," Liam said, coming over to sit next to me on the rock.

"No, it was because Owen is trying to prevent me from touching you."

Liam leaned closer. "You want to touch me again?" he asked in a husky, low voice that made me shiver.

"Ack!" Owen said.

"You can always leave," I suggested, looking back at Owen.

Owen floated closer to me and suddenly he was all seriousness. My smile dropped at his change of demeanor and I knew he was about to say something that would ruin my mood.

"You need to tell him about your roommate."

And with that my mood was officially ruined. All the warmth I felt before was replaced with fear and dread. Shawna's warning from earlier came to mind. I needed to tell them about the professional Templars coming to hunt us and the mark that all the dead had on their arms. I wanted to talk to Owen about it first, but it seemed as if I wouldn't get my chance. Gah! I was tired of all this and as soon as I said something, Liam would be back to his cold shoulder, bossy, Conquest self.

I sighed and nodded, acting as if I agreed with Owen, even though I planned to tell the guys only about the incoming threat not about Shawna. Then Owen disappeared leaving me alone with Liam.

Chapter 15

"He's gone," I told Liam.

Liam sighed. "I wish I could see him. I have so much I want to say."

I understood that. "Maybe next time I can be the medium like in one of those psychic shops."

Liam chuckled. "With the crazy robes and accent?"

"Definitely." I stood up and turned towards the trail that would lead me back to the bridge. "Ready to go?" I wished I could stay longer and figure out what this new thing was between Liam and I but there were more pressing matters that I needed to tell all three guys.

Liam nodded and grabbed my hand, leading me back the way we came. I did not hesitate this time at the bridge. I kept my eyes forward and walked as quickly as I could while trying not to sway the bridge too much. I made it to the other side without looking down and continued down the trail, remembering the rest of the way. By the time we made it to the bike I was exhausted. Liam had dried off for the most part by that point and put his shirt back on. I tried to hide my disappointment, but his grin told me he knew. Liam got onto his bike and was about to start it up, but I jumped forward and placed my hand on his arm to stop him.

Before the engine drowned out our words and before I ruined the day with my information, I wanted to know where that kiss left us. Were we friends? Something more? I hated to think it but a teeny, tiny part of me wondered if he had kissed me to manipulate me. To make me more open to following his orders. I instantly pushed that thought away, refusing to believe that he would do something so dastardly.

"Um, Liam, so, uh…what are we?" I wiggled my finger indicating the two of us.

He studied me as he grabbed the extra bike helmet and handed it to me. I waited patiently for him to say something but as the silence grew, my nerves grew with it. I tucked the helmet under my arm then fiddled with my bracelet while I waited for him to say something.

"I don't know," he finally said, looking away. "For the longest time you were my best friend's sister although I couldn't help liking you. You were always so confident, lively and didn't take shit from anyone, how could I not?"

My heart skipped a beat at his words. Liam had liked me in high school? I never picked up on that. Probably because of all the other girls he usually had hanging off him.

"Then Owen died." Liam closed his eyes as if forcing down an unwanted emotion. "And you became Death." He looked back at me and I saw anguish and struggle within his eyes. "I didn't know what to do to protect you except push you away, but you kept coming back. Every time you stood up to me made me want you more, but it was dangerous to have you near us."

I blushed and looked away, not wanting to be caught in his heated gaze. It was heartwarming to know he had liked me all along, even though he had a terrible way of showing it. I never admitted to anyone, not even Owen, but I had a crush on Liam in high school as well, and even though I hated seeing him when they showed up at orientation two months ago, I felt all those emotions again. However, it was pretty easy to ignore when Liam was being a jerk.

"So, what are we?" Liam shook his head and smiled. "I don't know, but if you're willing, I would like to find out."

My stomach fluttered and happiness swept through me. I jumped forward and kissed Liam, surprising us both. He chuckled and wrapped his arms around my waist.

"I have one condition though."

Of course, he did. I tensed, readying myself for a battle of wills. I would not be babied so he better not even think about it.

"You have to promise me you won't put yourself in danger."

I narrowed my eyes. "Are you giving me an ultimatum?" I tried to pull back, hurt that he would do something like that.

He tightened his hold around me, refusing to let me go. "No, I'm not giving you an ultimatum, but I will not be able to stay sane if you keep throwing yourself into dangerous situations. Every time I find you in danger I freak out and my talent goes wild."

I noticed he showed concern before, but I never knew he freaked out. Aw, he cared. However, I couldn't promise him what he wanted. All those times I found myself in danger were not my fault. I put my arms around his neck and leaned in.

"I will try but I can't promise anything."

He growled and I kissed him on his nose, then pulled out of his embrace. He let me go and sighed. I thought I heard him murmur something about being difficult and causing him to have a heart attack but he started up the engine at the same time so I couldn't be sure. I put my helmet on then got on the back of the bike and relaxed against Liam's back for the ride home.

We had been gone for most of the day, so I was surprised to find Kaden and Trevor still in front of the TV.

"Don't you guys have homework to do? Have you even moved?" I asked as I walked toward the kitchen to grab some lemonade.

"We are binge watching Lucifer," Kaden called out from the living room.

I chuckled and got out a glass. I felt someone behind me, but I didn't turn around, instead I got another glass and poured us both some lemonade. When I turned around, Liam was standing close. I held out a glass to him and he took it, smiling at me flirtatiously. I didn't return the smile which made him tilt his head questioningly.

I sighed and set my glass down at the table. "I've gotta talk to you guys," I said.

Liam's brows drew down silently asking what I needed to talk about.

I ignored his look and called to Trevor and Kaden.

"But we are at a really good part," Kaden called back.

I walked into the living room and grabbed the remote. Trevor jumped up to wrestle the remote from me before I could stop it, but he got to me too late. I pressed pause and exited out of Netflix. They glared at me but followed me back to the kitchen where Liam sat waiting.

"I need to talk to you guys about something serious."

That got their attention. I waited until we were all seated around the table then cupped my hands around the glass of lemonade, using it as a barrier between me and the three Horsemen.

"I came across some information recently about the Templars."

Liam narrowed his eyes at me, and I saw his hand tighten around his glass. I knew he was wondering why I hadn't told him anything earlier.

"I found out the Templars are sending some professionals to hunt us. They will be here within two weeks." I looked at Liam. "It looks like you were right about them blaming me for this outbreak." I bit my lip, waiting for their reactions.

They stared at me with varying degrees of disbelief and fear. Then all three of their expressions turned suspicious.

"How did you come across that information?" Liam asked.

His tone chilled me, and I felt sad to know the cold, vexed Liam was back. At least now I knew he did that because he was protective of me and he was guarding his emotions, but I still didn't like it.

"I would like to keep my sources confidential," I replied and winced at their instantaneous yelling.

They could yell all they wanted but Shawna was my secret and she had risked herself to bring me that information. There was no way I would throw her to the dogs, well, Horseman, after that. Even though I was still hurt by her lie of omission I wanted to believe her when she said I could trust her. She hadn't seen me as a threat when she knew I was a supposed Horseman, so I would give her a chance. I really hoped I didn't regret it.

Liam's voice rose above the others, quieting Trevor and Kaden. Liam pierced me with hard hazel-brown eyes, but I could see the hurt within them. I felt guilty that I was already keeping things from him, but I wasn't going to back down.

"Fine. But just know, I will find out," Liam warned.

He could try but unless Shawna or I told him he would never figure out that my information came from my ex-roommate. I shrugged. "It doesn't matter how I know; it matters that we are in danger. And there's another thing. All of the dead students had scythe marks on their arms." I bit my lip thinking over the implications. "I think someone is doing this and framing me."

Liam made a rumbling noise in his chest and his gaze stayed trained on me. He reminded me of a wolf. Hmm, were werewolves real? The Horseman couldn't be the only supernatural beings out there.

"You promised me," Liam said, bringing my focus back to the issue at hand.

I held up a finger. "Technically I didn't, but how is this my fault?" Once again, I didn't choose to be in dangerous situations but somehow there I was.

"Promised him what?" Kaden asked, reminding me there were two other people at the table.

I took my eyes away from Liam and looked at Trevor and Kaden. "Nothing. So, what are we going to do about these professionals and the person framing me?"

"There isn't much we can do. If we knew who they were then maybe we could find them before they found us," Kaden said, and looked at me expectantly.

I shook my head letting them know I didn't know who the hunters were. I just realized I didn't even know how many were coming or what to expect. I would have to contact Shawna later, once I had some privacy. This was going to cause so much paranoia.

"I don't think we should go to classes," Trevor announced.

I made a noise of protest. I had to go to classes or else I would fail, today did not count. It was only my first semester. I did not want to be part of the small percent that dropped out after their first semester because they couldn't handle it. I may be in danger, which is a better excuse than most, but dang it if I would let those Templars push me to failure because I was too paranoid to go outside.

"He's right, we don't know when or where this attack will happen or who to expect," Kaden said, siding with Trevor.

I shook my head vehemently. "I am going to classes. I am not failing. What would I tell my parents?"

"What would you tell them if you ended up dead?" Liam threw at me.

I flinched, knowing full well my death would destroy them especially since it was still relatively close to Owen's death. Still, my education was important, and I liked to think I would have a future, so I needed to prepare for that.

"Then maybe we should train more and use the buddy system," I suggested.

Kaden threw his hands up in exasperation while Trevor shook his head and grumbled.

"Seriously though, let's carry weapons and practice our talents." I knew there were some knives and daggers laying around here somewhere. I could just grab a few and hide them in my backpack.

Trevor and Kaden looked to Liam which made me look at him too. The three of us waited for his final order. Not that I would listen to him, but he was the leader and I knew Kaden and Trevor would do whatever he said, including locking me up if it came to that. I could tell Liam thought about the locking me up part and I narrowed my eyes silently telling him to unthink it.

Liam frowned and his jaw tightened. "You are still going to leave the house to go to class no matter what we say, huh?"

I smiled mischievously. "You're learning," I playfully praised.

Liam pinched the bridge of his nose. "Fine, we will use the buddy system. Kaden and Trevor together, and me and Phi. I will investigate and try to figure out who is framing Phi."

Kaden and Trevor started to protest but Liam shook his head and they fell silent.

"I will grab the weapons," Trevor said resigned, and got up to go get them.

"I will set up a training schedule, I guess," Kaden said and walked upstairs to his room.

"You know, I could probably rig some booby traps for the house," I suggested, wanting to help in some way.

Liam nodded in agreement then stood up. "Do. Not. Leave this house without me," Liam warned, making sure to emphasize the first two words, then walked out of the kitchen.

By the end of the week I was absolutely exhausted. When Kaden said he would create a new schedule I didn't think I would be training during every single free moment. If I wasn't creating booby traps, doing homework, or attending class, then I was swinging a scythe, throwing daggers and punches, and practicing my talents which thankfully were getting stronger now that I knew how to use them. All I had to do now was think about loss and how it made me feel and I could cause anyone in the room to feel sick. Not collapse and puke your guts out sick. I could cause puke level sick when I actually touched them. I have nightmares about the things I've seen from their stomachs.

I also experienced high levels of the others' talents. I do not think I have ever felt more anger, despair, and fear in my whole life. However, the more I felt their talents the more I could conjure up my own since it drew on those three. It had become a battle between Liam and I on who could cause the other to cave first. Unfortunately, I had been the one to tap out each time since his talent was so strong and he was Conquest, meaning he had a natural advantage in anything. The only way I would win was if I decided to use pestilence and I was not planning on killing my maybe boyfriend anytime soon.

I was sitting across from Kaden, trying to make him sick without touching him, when I had a thought.

"Does Death cause a general illness, or can I differentiate between viruses?" I figured Kaden would be the best one to ask since he was our unofficial scholar on all things Horsemen.

"What do you mean?" He asked distractedly. I sent another wave of my talent at him, and I knew it hit when he frowned and bent forward slightly. His green eyes darkened. He was good at hiding it, but I had gotten used to his tells enough to know he was feeling it.

"Well right now you probably feel nauseous, but that is not really apocalyptic level talent. As Death, can I pick, like the flu or Ebola, to spread?" I withdrew my power to let Kaden breathe easier and respond.

Kaden took a moment to catch his breath and straighten then tilted his head in thought. "I don't see why not. You are the actual, real life Death, a sign of the apocalypse according to many myths so it would make sense that you control all sorts of diseases." Kaden eyed me as if looking for something. "You aren't thinking of doing anything crazy are you?"

My eyes widened in horror. "What? No! I'm not going to become some kind of terrorist, calm down." I shrugged and looked down at my hands. "I was just wondering."

Kaden stayed quiet a bit longer then stood up abruptly. I looked up at him, wondering if practice was over already. That would be nice. Maybe I could finally have a bit of down time. He held out his hand and I took it, letting him pull me up.

"I want to show you something," he said, and walked toward the stairs.

Curious about what it was, I followed him. Upstairs we passed the guest room and I thought about darting inside so I could relax for a while. Instead I continued down the hall behind Kaden. I expected Trevor or Liam to come out of their rooms, but their doors stayed closed.

At the end of the hall he stopped in front of a door that I knew led to his room. "You can come in here anytime you want." He chuckled and his cheeks reddened a bit. "Well, knock first."

I opened my mouth to ask him why I would want to go in there, but my words died when he opened the door and I saw what was inside.

Chapter 16

My eyes widened and I gasped, trying to take everything in. I took a few steps into the room and turned in a slow circle to get a better look. Covering every wall except the one his bed was against were bookshelves filled with books. His whole room was a mini library and I instantly knew I would be coming back often. On display on some of the bookshelves were various daggers and other weapons. Behind his bed, on the wall, hung an ancient looking sword which I suspected to be the original sword of the first War Horseman, just like my scythe was the one Death first used.

I went up to one of the shelves and ran my finger over some of the spines. Old books were interspersed among newer ones, but all were dusted and clean. After reading some of the titles, I could tell there was a theme. Kaden confirmed it a second later when he came to stand beside me.

"All these books are on the apocalypse. Not just the Christian version but I have the Egyptian, Norse, and Aztec versions as well as others."

I stared in wonder at all the books. I never knew there were so many stories about the end of the world. I turned to look at the other bookcases and nodded my head towards them. "What about those?"

Kaden turned to look at them with me. "I have a section for each of the Horsemen." He walked over to the nearest bookcase and held out his hand as if presenting it. "This one is all about War, including mythologies from different cultures about war stuff. Even if it doesn't mention the Horsemen specifically, I have books about similar aspects."

I looked at the other bookshelves in the room. "Where is mine?" It felt so weird to know that a whole bookcase was dedicated to the Death Horseman which happened to be me and my predecessors. It made me shiver.

He walked down the line of bookshelves, pointing to each one. "This one is Conquest's, this one Famine, and this one is yours."

The bookcase holding at least a hundred books about Death, pestilence or anything similar sat along the wall opposite the door. I looked at the last bookcase next to mine, which was positioned near the bed and was only half the size of the others.

I pointed to it. "What about that one?"

Kaden cleared his throat making me look at him in curiosity. His cheeks reddened a bit and he refused to look me in the eyes. "Those, uh, are my personal books."

A smile crept up on my face. "You read for fun?"

Kaden looked offended. "Yes, and it is actually quite fun thank you very much."

I held up my hands. "Whoa, I'm not judging, just curious." I walked over to his little bookshelf, passing mine along the way and stooped down to see the titles. "Ok now I'm judging. You like romance books?"

I glanced up at Kaden who had followed me and saw him blush harder. The red in his cheeks made the orange highlights in his russet hair stand out. It was actually kind of adorable.

"Now I know why you're such a good flirt."

Kaden turned his back to me and grumbled. "Shut up."

I laughed at his reaction and walked over to my bookshelf, letting his reading habits go for now. "Wow," I breathed, gazing at the multitude of books on the shelves.

There were more books about death and the practices surrounding it than Conquest or Famine had about their topics. War may have been close since every culture ever dealt with war. There were so many books about death that it seemed impossible to ever get through it all.

"Like I said, you can come in here anytime to study these. I haven't found anything yet about your ghost thing, but we can look together, and this would also be the best place to research the extent of your talent," Kaden said from behind me.

I turned around with a huge grin. "Thanks." I meant it too. I loved looking through books to research things which is why I liked studying at the library but ever since I had been attacked there I hadn't gone back. Now I had a place to go to find out information about all this Horsemen stuff especially since Shawna's Bible did not explain enough.

My cell phone rung making us both jump. I fished it out of my pocket and checked the screen. Shawna. Speak of the devil, well, Templar.

I answered it and moved toward the door so Kaden couldn't overhear. I kept my eyes on him to make sure he didn't come near me and answered the phone. "Yes?" I said making sure to keep the frown from my face in case Kaden questioned me about it.

"They're coming," Shawna said sending chills down my arms.

Fear tried to tighten my chest, but I took deep breaths to calm myself. "When?" Yes! I managed to keep my voice steady. Take that, fear.

"Soon, I don't know. There is a meeting about it tomorrow night." Shawna sounded a bit scared which only made me feel even more uneasy.

I glanced at Kaden who tried to act like he wasn't listening to me by messing with some of the books on his bookshelves. I made sure to lower my voice. "Can you come here so we can talk in person."

A pause on the other line made me think she would say no. Instead she said, "Sure, I will be over in a few minutes." Then she hung up.

I put my phone away and Kaden immediately asked, "What was that about?"

"Nothing. Shawna is coming over to give me something." I made sure to keep my voice even and look nonchalant.

Kaden stood up straighter and his eyes flitted around. "Shawna is coming over?"

I narrowed my eyes at him. Did the War Horseman have a crush on my Templar ex-roommate? Not that he knew of her identity but still, I would have to make sure he didn't get anywhere near her. I blinked in bewilderment when I realized I didn't want to keep her away for Kaden's safety but rather hers.

I pointed my finger at him and scolded him like he was a puppy. "No, you stay away from her. She doesn't need any of your flirting or romance novel pickup lines."

His cheeks reddened and I found that making him blush was my new favorite hobby, well that and pushing Liam's buttons.

He waved his hands at the door, shooing me away. "Get out of here."

I chuckled at him as I left then made my way downstairs to wait for Shawna. My humor died when I remembered what she was coming over to talk about. I kept my phone gripped in my hand waiting for her to call and change her mind. I wouldn't blame her but if she did change her mind, I was going to pester her until she told me everything she knew. A few minutes later, a loud knocking at the door made me jump and almost drop my phone. I put it back in my pocket and took a deep breath then opened the door coming face to face with Shawna.

She looked around the area before meeting my eyes and waving with a tight-lipped smile. She looked nervous and a little jumpy. I hoped the Templars did not know she was here. I glanced around the house to make sure there were no Horsemen nearby then went outside, closing the door behind me. I crossed my arms over my chest, partly to show her I was still a little upset and partly to fend off the chill in the air.

"When and where is the meeting?" I asked, getting straight to the point.

Shawna glanced around again making sure we were truly alone. "Tomorrow night, 6pm in a community center. The university chapter house where the Penn State Templars live is too small to accommodate everyone. We have our meetings at the center occasionally when the Pennsylvania chapter comes to the school."

"Why don't you live with them?" I asked. She had been in the dorms since the first day, yet she could have lived in a nice off campus chapter house.

Shawna sighed. "I already told you. They wanted me to live with you and report any findings. They had to make sure you were who they thought you were before they made a move." At my suspicious look Shawna held up her hands. "I swear I never told them anything."

I nodded, deciding to believe her. She had been giving me information which was risky when her Order was into killing people. I wasn't ready to admit it out loud, but I had slowly been trusting her again and thinking of her as a sort of friend. Maybe it was because I hadn't had a friend in a long time, and I was a little desperate for one that wasn't a machine. The friends I had in high school stopped hanging around me because I became depressed and withdrawn after Owen's death and I had pushed away Liam, Kaden, and Trevor who tried to stick by my side.

"I will tell you what they say right after the meeting," Shawna said quietly.

"No." I had a sudden absolutely crazy idea and Liam was not going to like it.

"No?" she asked bewildered. "Why?"

"I want to go to the meeting." I almost took it back as soon as it left my lips, but I clenched my fists and bit my tongue. I wanted to go and hear what they had to say for myself. I wanted to know how many Templars there were and see their faces. I was tired of being attacked by strangers. At least this way I would recognize them first. Maybe I would find out who had been framing me and put a stop to it before they killed any more people. And they said the Horsemen were evil. I snorted and shook my head at the thought.

Shawna shook her head with wide eyes. "No, you can't go. They will recognize you."

I huffed, realizing she was right. Then I snapped my fingers as an idea hit me. "I could wear a wig and disguise myself." Yeah, that would totally work.

She gave me a look like I was an idiot. "This is not a movie, Phi."

I rolled my eyes. "I know that, Shawna. C'mon it's a good idea. You could get me a wig and it will be fine."

Shawna opened her mouth to argue, frowning as she did in disapproval, but the door opened, and Kaden poked his head out forcing her to hold off on what she was going to say.

"Shawna! So nice to see you."

Shawna's face morphed from serious to flirty in an instant. I had to blink a few times to get on track with the new atmosphere. I glared at Kaden trying to silently tell him to go away. He glanced at me and smiled, completely ignoring my order.

"We were planning on having a movie night. Why don't you stay?" Kaden suggested, looking hopeful.

Movie night? Since when? I started to protest but Shawna spoke up first. "I would love that, thank you."

"Great, I will tell the others." Kaden went back into the house leaving Shawna and I alone.

I switched my narrowed eyes from the door where Kaden had stood to Shawna. "What was that?" I accused.

Shawna looked at me innocently though I could tell she knew what I was talking about. "What do you mean?"

I walked up to her so I could speak low and show her how serious I was. "You guys can't be together. You can come in just this once but don't think it will happen again." I know that sounded mean, but I was trying to protect Kaden and Shawna. "Also, bring me the wig tomorrow."

Before she could refuse, I walked into the house but not before I saw the hurt look on her face. My chest pinched with guilt. Maybe I had been unnecessarily harsh. I wouldn't take it back though. Shawna was a Templar and Kaden was the War Horseman. That just spelled trouble.

Shawna walked in after me a second later with no trace of the hurt she showed a moment before. Instead, she had a bright smile plastered on her face which got wider when she spotted Kaden. Annoyingly, Kaden's smile turned just as bright when he saw her, and he came over to guide her to a seat in the living room. They started talking and laughing as Kaden pulled up Netflix. I kept my eyes on them and crossed my arms. What could they possibly be talking about?

"Why are you frowning?" a deep voice said in my ear.

I jumped, nearly cracking my head on the person and turned to the owner of the voice. I hit Liam on the arm for scaring me, but he only chuckled and captured my hand, then guided me to the kitchen.

"You're going to help me make dinner," he said. I raised an eyebrow even though he couldn't see it since he was in front of me. "Oh, I am, am I?"

He turned and sighed, looking up at the ceiling as if exasperated then he looked back at me with raised eyebrows and false sincerity. "Phi? Can you please help me make dinner?"

One side of my mouth pulled up at his attempt at good manners and humility. "Well, since you asked so nicely, sure."

"Good." He dropped the false politeness and turned around to pull out pots and pans. "Get the ingredients for spaghetti."

I rolled my eyes at his bossy tone but smiled and did as he ordered. We worked together to make enough food for five people including grating cheese and baking garlic bread. When it was all done, we set it out on the table and called everyone to the kitchen.

Trevor came in almost immediately as if he had been standing by the kitchen waiting for us to call him. He was always on board to eat although his vegetarian choices made us have to keep the meat separate from the noodles. Shawna and Kaden came in next and I was perturbed to see Kaden standing so close to her. Shawna leaned back into him a little and I narrowed my eyes at her letting her know I noticed. She shrugged at me and sat down, looking over the dishes we prepared. Once everyone was seated, we dug in.

It was nice to sit at the table together, not as supernatural people, but as friends and have a good meal. Shawna being there made me a bit nervous and I kept glancing at the others wondering if they would figure out that she was a Templar, but nothing happened. I started to relax and smile more, happy that I could take a break from training and just enjoy the night.

After everyone was full, I stood up and touched my nose. "Nose goes on dishes," I announced. I did not want to wash them since I cooked and thought this would be a fun way to force someone else to do it.

Shawna, Kaden, and Liam immediately touched their noses and smiled at the silly game. Trevor was a second too late and we all burst into laughter at his loss.

"Thanks Trevor," Kaden said, getting up from the table and handing his plate over to Trevor.

Trevor snatched it and grumbled while he collected the other dishes. I left Trevor to clean up and followed the others to the living room, wondering what movie they planned on watching. I expected something scary, with action, or at the very least rated R. The guys just seemed like the kind of people that would enjoy those movies. Instead when I walked into the living room, I saw Frozen queued up.

I stared in shock at the TV then glanced at the others wondering if they were serious. That's when I noticed the arguing. Kaden wrestled with Shawna on the couch, trying to get the remote from her while shouting about her terrible movie choices. She argued back by singing the main song in Frozen, Let It Go. Liam stood by with crossed arms, and a small smile, watching the fight that was happening on the couch. I shared a look of amusement with him then went over to break up the fight. I managed to get the remote away from Shawna and jumped back before either of them could snatch it from me. I pointed at them and raised my eyebrows in warning.

Once I knew they were calm, though I had to squeeze my lips together to hold in my laughter at their messy state, I said, "Ok, how about we vote on what to watch?"

Shawna bit her bottom lip to stop smiling and glanced at Kaden who glared at the TV. "I vote Frozen," she said.

"I am not watching Frozen," Kaden responded, crossing his arms in finality. He fought a smile that threatened to disrupt his grumpy face letting me know he was not mad and actually found the whole situation amusing.

I shook my head at them and looked to Liam. "What do you want to watch?"

Liam shrugged a shoulder, "I don't care."

I shrugged back and held up the remote to press play though I knew Liam would stop me. I was just trying to mess with him and Kaden. "Then I guess we will watch Frozen."

"Whoa, wait, no. Not that." Liam stepped toward me and held out a hand to stop me from pressing play.

Shawna burst into laughter on the couch. Trevor came in and looked at all of us and frowned. "What's going on?" He walked over to Kaden and plopped onto the end of the couch.

"We are trying to find a movie to watch," Kaden explained.

Trevor looked at the TV and his eyes widened when he saw it was Frozen. "You guys didn't choose that, did you?"

That caused everyone to laugh but Trevor only looked at us with more confusion which made me laugh so hard I had tears running down my face.

"Give me that," Liam grumbled when his laughter died down and took the remote from my hands. I was too weak from laughing to resist so I let him have it.

He went to the search menu and put in a different title. When Kaden and Trevor saw what he was searching for they voiced their support. I rolled my eyes and went to sit on the floor in front of Shawna's legs, since the couch had no more open spots.

When Liam pressed play on the Fast and the Furious he came to sit beside me and nudged my shoulder with his. I looked up at him and my breath caught at the genuine smile on his face. He had not smiled like that in a while and I was suddenly grateful Kaden had put this together, even if it was spur of the moment.

It was nice for us to all have a night of no worries and just hang out together as friends.

Chapter 17

We ended up watching the sequel afterwards and it was nearly midnight by the time the second movie ended. Shawna, Kaden and Trevor passed out on the couch with Shawna's head leaning against Kaden's shoulder. Liam and I had gone to our rooms afterward leaving the three of them there.

When I went downstairs the next morning, Shawna was gone, and Kaden cuddled Trevor's arm. I took out my phone and quickly snapped a picture of them, wanting to use it later to tease them. Once I got the picture, I texted it to Shawna then asked her where she went. While I waited for her reply, I quietly made my way to the kitchen to find something to eat. Thankfully it was the weekend, so I did not need to rush to class.

My phone buzzed with a notification. I checked it and smiled at her laughing emoji. Then she said that she went home to prepare for tonight. That made my smile die instantly. Dang, I had almost forgotten about the meeting.

I needed to tell the guys about it. I sent a text reminding her to get me a wig then put my phone down to make us all some breakfast.

"What is that delicious smell?" I heard Trevor ask from behind me.

I chuckled and moved aside so he could see what I was making. Bacon sizzled in a pan while chocolate chip pancakes cooked in another. Trevor inhaled and hummed in approval, although I knew he wouldn't eat the bacon. He moved to a cabinet and started pulling out plates for all of us. Kaden joined us a few minutes later, his hair looking rumpled, but it only made him look cuter. If Shawna were here, she probably would have been eyeing him hungrily. I laughed to myself at the thought.

"What's so funny?" Kaden asked, coming to stand behind me and peer over my shoulder at the food.

I didn't want to tell him about my thoughts, instead I pulled out my phone and brought up the picture of him cuddling Trevor's arm. I held it up over my head so he could see it while I flipped pancakes with my other hand. I fought a grin when he snatched the phone from me and shouted in dismay.

"What is it?" I heard Trevor ask.

I still didn't turn around, trying even harder to hold in my laughter. I cracked some eggs in another pan and looked over the bacon, but Trevor's shocked gasp nearly undid me. I snickered, not able to hold in my amusement completely but reigned it in just as fast.

"Dude, what were you doing?" Trevor asked. I heard a thwack and Kaden grumbled.

Kaden showed up in my line of sight holding my phone with one hand and his head that Trevor must have hit with the other. "No one else sees this, understand?"

I gave him a fake apologetic look. "Oops, I kinda already showed Shawna."

Kaden's cheeks turned red. "You did what?" He sighed and rubbed his forehead, grumbling. Then he put my phone on the counter and walked away.

"Breakfast is ready!" I announced.

The three of us ate silently at the table, Kaden occasionally shooting me a dark look which only made me smile wide in return. Liam came into the kitchen when we were wrapping up our meal. I pointed to the stove to show him there was some left. He nodded and quietly plated some food, and sat down to eat, sticking with the silent atmosphere by not saying a word.

I collected our plates and set them in the sink when everyone was completely finished. I quickly turned back to the table and opened my mouth to stop them from leaving so I could tell them about the Templar meeting tonight, but the words got stuck in my throat. If I told them I was going then they would probably throw me in a closet again to stop me. If we were going to learn anything firsthand, then someone needed to be there, and I had already decided that someone would be me. If I somehow convinced them to let me go then they would insist on joining me. That would be terrible because they would find out the identity of my informant.

I glanced at Liam knowing he would be furious when he found out later, but I closed my mouth anyway and decided not to tell them. I could explain afterwards and hopefully they won't be as mad when I bring back useful information. In order to be prepared tonight, I needed weapons and information about the Templars. Kaden probably had both.

I changed gears and headed towards the stairs, calling over my shoulder to Kaden, "I'm going to get some books from your room." I didn't wait for a response.

In Kaden's room, I went straight to the bookcase about Death and pulled a couple promising books out. I really wanted to know if I could isolate certain diseases when I used my talent. Not that I would use them on innocent people but being knowledgeable about an apocalyptic level power would be useful. I wandered around the room looking for books about the Templars but as time went on, I got more and more frustrated that I couldn't find any.

"Looking for anything specific?" Kaden asked from the doorway.

I jumped a little and glared at him for scaring me. "Knock next time," I grumbled.

Kaden smirked. "This is my room." He walked farther into the room and looked over the books I already pulled from the shelves.

I looked around, remembering it was indeed his room, and nodded. "Right, sorry." I went back to the shelf and ran my fingers over titles. "Do you have anything about the Templars?"

I turned to look at Kaden when he moved across the room to another bookshelf. "Sorta, I have information on the Inquisition and Popes but nothing specific about the Order of Templars. They are super secretive." He pulled one book from the War section and one from the Conquest section then laid them on top of my pile of books I gathered. "Anything else?"

"Nope, thanks." I quickly gathered the five books and rushed to my room, eager to start researching.

Something buzzed near my head. When I ignored it, the buzzing started again. Groaning, I opened my eyes and peeled my cheek away from the page in the book I rested it on after many hours of reading. The buzzing happened again and this time I recognized it as my phone with an incoming call. The caller ID showed Shawna's name and I was instantly wide awake. I scrambled for the phone and pressed answer before she gave up.

"Hello?" My voice came out groggy, so I cleared my throat and tried again. "Shawna?"

"Girl, I was about to go without you," she said exasperated.

"Sorry." I pulled the phone back from my ear enough to see the time then put it back. "Wow, it's nearly six already. Are you on your way over?"

There was a pause. "Yes," she said reluctantly, "Even though, I don't think you should go."

"See you soon," I said, ignoring her latter comment.

I hung up and put the book away that I had been reading and ended up falling asleep on. I tugged on a leather jacket with inside pockets and put boots on. I looked like a badass but the real reason I wore those was for extra hiding places. I tucked a pocketknife in my jeans pocket, a small dagger in each boot, and a can of pepper spray and brass knuckles in my inside jacket pockets. If I could have carried my scythe somehow without it being seen I would have brought that too since I was pretty good at using it now that I had training with it. I tied my dark hair back so that the wig could be placed on my head easier. Once I felt ready, I went downstairs. I still didn't know what I was going to tell the guys about where I was going but I would wing it.

I almost made it to the door before Liam's voice called out stopping me in my tracks. "Where are you going?"

I slowly turned around and plastered a bright, hopefully innocent, smile on my face. "Out."

He raised an eyebrow at my answer and crossed his arms waiting for me to elaborate. I nodded and looked around, trying to avoid eye contact and fiddled with my bracelet. It was a standoff now of who could stay silent the longest. However, I didn't have time for that.

I broke the silence after a minute. "Well, good talk. Bye." I turned and opened the door, but a strong arm suddenly appeared, blocking my way.

"Where are you going?" he repeated.

Thankfully, Shawna showed up on the front porch with a grocery bag in one hand, acting as the perfect distraction. "Shawna!" I darted under his arm and reached out to my ex-roommate.

"Uh, hi," she said, glancing from me to Liam then frowned at me curiously.

Liam stepped out onto the porch and crossed his arms, eyeing both of us suspiciously.

A lie sprung to mind and I went with it, hoping it would work. It worked in books and movies so it must be true. Right? "Shawna was bringing me, um, some uh," I lowered my voice to a whisper, "lady supplies. If you know what I mean."

If I wasn't trying so hard to act truthful, I would have cracked up at the blush that colored Liam's cheeks. The big, bad Horseman was embarrassed by some lady things. Just what I wanted but I didn't expect it to actually work. I raised my eyebrows at Shawna, silently urging her to play along.

"Uh, yeah, I got 'em right here." Shawna raised the bag in the air.

Liam looked at the bag and blushed harder. He cleared his throat and looked anywhere but us or the bag. "Well, I guess I will leave you to it." He quickly made his escape back into the house.

Once I knew he was gone and couldn't hear us I snatched the bag from Shawna. "Hurry, let's go before he checks on me."

We hurried from the porch and I let her lead the way. As we walked, I pulled out a short blonde wig from the bag. "Blonde? Really?"

Shawna snorted a laugh. "I didn't expect you to be picky about a wig."

I stuck my tongue out causing her to laugh then put the wig on over my dark hair. The important thing was to hide my white streaks of hair because that drew too much attention.

"I also have something else for you."

I looked at her curiously wondering what else she had gotten. As long as it helped me go unnoticed, I was on board. She grabbed the bag from me and pulled out a container of…something. I honestly had no idea what I was looking at.

"They're contacts," Shawna explained after I stared at the thing blankly.

"Pshh, I don't need contacts, I have great vision." I shooed away the container in her hand.

She held them out to me, shaking them a little to get me to take them. "They're color contacts. Brown to be exact. The idea is to hide your white streaks and pale eyes. Those are too unique to go unnoticed."

"Ah, smart!" I took them and opened the container where two brown lenses laid. "How do I put them in?"

Shawna showed me and soon I had brown eyes and short blonde hair. I didn't feel any different, but Shawna's thumbs up told me I looked different. Good, now time to crash a meeting.

The community center where the meeting would be held looked so innocent. I was pretty sure I had passed by it a few times, but never did I realize Templars congregated there.

Shawna pushed me behind her, so I was mostly hidden, and we snuck inside, skirting along the edge until we took some seats in the back. No one gave us a second look, but I continued to hold my breath until we were seated. There were already thirty or so others in attendance and I took a good look at each of their faces, trying to memorize them for the future.

Shawna leaned over so she could speak without being heard by the others. "The meeting should start soon." She nodded to a group of people at the front of the room. "Those three up there are the leaders of the Templars in Pennsylvania." She nodded to a group sitting a couple rows in front of us. "And those four are the last Penn State Templars. Well, besides me."

I stared at the Penn State Templars, although I could only see the backs of their heads at the moment. I had killed one of them and felt horrible about it, even though she instigated the fight. They probably were not too happy about it either way. Maybe one of them was the framer. My eyes zeroed in on one individual and my breath caught. It was the blonde Templar from the library. I had completely forgotten about him. I shrunk down in my seat a little more, not wanting to draw his attention. If there was a chance, he would be the only one to recognize me other than Shawna.

Shawna saw where my eyes had landed and whispered, "That is the brother of the Templar that you, um, killed."

My head spun around to stare at her with shock. He was the brother of the girl I killed? Great, now he had even more of a reason to hurt me. Oh my goodness! What if he was the framer? He was my number one suspect now, so I had to figure out a way to find out more about him. I started to ask about him when the leaders of the Pennsylvania Templars called for our attention. I shut my mouth and looked to the front where the three leaders sat at a head table.

One was an older man, probably in his forties, with a round face, brown hair and brown eyes. He looked normal and I would never have suspected him as a cult leader. A woman sat next to him, about the same age, maybe a little older if the gray in her blonde hair was any indication. She had dark eyes and tanned skin. She stared out over the crowd with an emotionless face. The guy next to her was the oldest. He also looked to be the one in charge, like the head honcho. He smiled at some people in the front row and looked innocent enough. He was probably in his seventies with short gray hair, wrinkles, big chin, and blue eyes. Although, he wore a traditional robe that made him look the part of a cult leader.

"We have some very important news," the oldest man in the robe announced. That quieted everyone down.

"As you all know, after the death of one of our own and of many innocent college students we have decided to bring in professionals before this mess escalates," the woman added.

My cheeks burned with guilt. I didn't mean to kill the college guy at the party or the Templar girl. In addition to feeling guilty about the loss of control over my powers I also felt offended. They brought in professionals, so my "mess" didn't escalate? They attacked me first! The second body never would have happened if they didn't try killing me and the rest of the bodies were not my fault. I eyed the blonde college Templar to see his reaction then gave up when the back of his head revealed nothing.

Shawna squeezed my arm briefly before letting go. I nodded at her show of comfort and calmed down a bit.

"We would like you all to meet them tonight." The plain man on the end stood up and walked over to the door, opening it then escorting three men inside.

I shot a wide-eyed look at Shawna. She never mentioned they would be here tonight. A hint of betrayal wormed its way into my mind, but I squashed it. Shawna did not betray me. She looked just as shocked as I was that they were there. She gripped my arm again but this time it was not comforting due to the panic she radiated.

The plain man waved the three professionals forward to say a little something then sat down, letting them take the stage. During my research, the closest thing I could get to figuring out the roles of the professionals was the history of the Inquisition. In the 12th century, the Inquisition rooted out heresy by torturing people and hunting down those they believed were against the Church. Their methods were terrifying, and no one was safe. They also had a part in witch hunts since witches were considered heretics. From that information I figured they must have included Horsemen into that mix and hunted them as well.

The men standing up front looked nothing like the books described. They all wore jeans and hiking boots. The one on the left was no more than thirty years old and had a plaid shirt on. In addition to his shirt and boots, his beard and mustache made him look like a lumberjack. The man in the middle was older with slick backed black hair and glasses. He looked so normal, almost like a professor. I shivered, thinking he might actually be a professor and I made a mental note to find out if he taught at Penn State so I could avoid his classes. The last guy was around my age and had a gauge in one ear, a nose piercing, and a band T-shirt. I never would have pegged him as a Templar let alone a professional, killer one.

The professor looking one stepped forward and addressed the people in the room. "Hello, it is nice to be in Pennsylvania, it has been a while since I've been here." He turned slightly and pointed to his colleagues. "This is Peter, Dean, and I am John. We will eradicate the threat and be gone before you know it."

The audience clapped and whistled. Trying to blend in, I did a soft, slow clap though my stomach twisted. All these people were clapping for my demise. Shivers skated down my arms when I imagined them figuring out I was in their midst.

John patted the air to let us know we should quiet down. "In order to help us deal with this efficiently, please answer any and all questions we may have for you." He sought out the Penn State university kids and nodded at them to let them know he would be seeking them out later. "Otherwise, please stay out of our way." With that, John waved to Peter and Dean to follow him and they took seats in the front row.

The old man in the robe took over again and adjourned the meeting a few minutes later. I darted for the door wanting to escape the room where three hunters were planning to kill me and my friends. I didn't wait to see if Shawna was behind me. All I could think about was getting as far away as I could from John, Peter, and Dean.

I almost made it until a hand reached out and gripped my arm, pulling me to a stop.

"Can I ask you a few questions?"

I turned, trying to keep the panic from my face. Dean, the professional Horseman hunter with the nose ring and gauge in his ear, held my arm as he looked at me expectantly. If I didn't know who he was I would think he was cute but I did know who he was and all I could imagine was him reaching into his jacket pocket, pulling out a dagger and stabbing me right there in front of the whole room.

"Um…" My mind blanked. I had to get out of there. Now!

I felt the stirrings of my talent kicking in and I had to focus all my energy in pushing it down, so I didn't accidentally kill the guy. Images of the Inquisition questioning and torturing people popped into my mind. That would be a big nope for me. I knew it was the 21st century and they probably didn't do things like that anymore but I was a Horseman hiding in plain sight while the big, scary Templar wanted to question me so sue me for thinking that was the way it would go.

Dean opened his mouth to say something. Maybe something like 'Hey are you a Horseman?' but he didn't get a chance. Shawna appeared on my left and took my arm from Dean's grasp. Dean glanced at the arm that escaped his grip then narrowed his eyes at Shawna.

"Hi, sorry, my friend only speaks Italian," Shawna covered, then tried to tug me away.

I shot a wide-eyed look at my friend, yes, I just referred to her as friend, we are good now, and shook my head the tiniest bit. I didn't know Italian.

She pursed her lips and nodded, wanting me to go along with it. Hopefully Dean didn't see that quick exchange. "She is an exchange student." Shawna almost had me to the door until Dean stopped her by tugging on my other arm, bringing us both back to stand in front of him.

I played along and tilted my head in confusion, acting like I couldn't understand their conversation.

Dean leveled his gaze back on me and smiled, but its fake appearance made dread pound in my chest. "Posso farti qualche domanda?"

I stared at him blankly. Crap. Of course, he spoke Italian. I shot a panicked look to Shawna. Her parents were in Italy, maybe she knew what Dean said. Shawna just stared back with an equally panicked look. I decided to wing it then get out of there fast.

I chuckled awkwardly and shook my head, looking apologetic. "Lo siento, tengo que ir." Italian was like Spanish, right? I took a couple Spanish classes in high school, so I knew how to say sorry and I have to go.

Dean chuckled, but his grip tightened on my arm, and his smile turned cold. "Nice try, but that was Spanish." He brought me closer and glared at me. "Who are you?"

Chapter 18

I opened my mouth to say no entiendo, sticking with my Spanish theme but the words never left my lips. The doors crashed open and all heads spun to see what caused it. Dean's hand loosened on my arm giving me the opportunity to yank it free. I gasped when Liam, Trevor, and Kaden walked in with confused expressions on their faces. They looked around then seemed to notice what this meeting was about, and their faces morphed into terrifying expressions that froze everyone to their spot.

I was relieved to see them. Together we could get out of this and I would be able to tell them about the professionals. I went to take a step toward them. As soon as I twitched and placed one foot forward, Liam's burning, hate filled eyes locked on me. Hurt spiked in my chest at the lack of recognition and hate that I saw there. He took another step into the room. He looked to be on the verge of murder.

A shocked gasp made me move my eyes away from Liam to Kaden. Kaden didn't look at me, instead he looked passed me with hurt and confusion flashing across his face. Eventually his features settled into fury and he took a step forward with clenched fists. I glanced behind me to see what made him react that way and saw Shawna shaking her head with tears in her eyes. I stepped back and gripped Shawna's hand letting her know I wouldn't let them hurt her.

"Where is she?" Liam shouted out at the Templars.

John came out of the crowd and faced the Horsemen with a smirk. "Well, well, well, thank you for saving us the trouble of hunting you down." John flicked his wrist down and a long blade materialized.

I jumped in shock at the sudden appearance of the blade. I wanted to learn that trick! Too bad he was a professional hunter and would kill me at his earliest convenience. I pulled Shawna away discreetly, not wanting to be in the line of John or Dean's attack.

"Where is she?" Liam repeated, ignoring the sword John now held.

The other Templars in the room shook off their shock and stepped up to stand behind John. Peter moved through the crowd until it was him, John, and Dean facing the Horsemen with the other Templars behind them.

Jeez, this was going to get ugly. Tension hung in the air and I braced myself for what was about to go down. My main goal was to get Shawna out of there then I could worry about getting the Horsemen and running away. That may make me sound like a coward but there was no way we could take on thirty Templars who had it out for us. The guys seemed to think they could because a second after I had that thought, the three of them launched themselves at the professionals. Chaos ensued and I had to dart to the side as a body went sailing through the air and landed where I had been standing.

I pulled on Shawna's hand and we made our way to the door that was no longer blocked by three angry Horsemen. Screams erupted in the crowd sending chills down my arms. I risked a look at the fight and saw Liam gripping a man's arm while the man screamed and tried to scramble away. The people in a five-foot radius of him gave him a wide berth as they struggled with their fear.

An almost inhuman roar made my head swivel to the other side of the room to find Kaden red faced and shouting at his opponents as he swung a sword at a Templar's head. The Templar turned out to be Peter who was just as angry. However, the more Peter got mad the stronger Kaden would become as he fed off his emotion. Kaden missed slicing Peter's head off but couldn't try again as three other Templars advanced on him. Kaden stood still and I almost felt the pulse of anger explode from him. The result was terrifying. The three men around Kaden shouted and turned on each other in a fit of rage. I almost stopped my progression to the door to stand and gape at the display of power.

I couldn't see Trevor anywhere, but I had no doubt he was using his ability to make his opponents feel weak and unable to fight as despair crashed through them. Hmm, maybe we could take on thirty Templars after all. I never realized how powerful the guys were. No wonder the Templars were afraid of us and wanted us dead.

I pulled Shawna the last few feet to the door and opened it. Suddenly the door was yanked from my hand as someone kicked it closed. I hissed at the stinging it left on my palm and turned to face our threat, moving Shawna behind me so I could protect her. I dropped into a guarded stance that Kaden taught me and pulled out a pocketknife from my jeans.

I relaxed when I saw it was Liam that stopped me. I lowered my weapon and smiled at him.

"No one leaves," he stated with clenched fists by his sides. His expression was guarded and cold. No hint of recognition or forgiveness in his eyes. It hurt more than being stabbed.

I took a step toward him to explain how sorry I was for not telling him I went to the meeting, but his gasp stopped me.

His eyes focused on Shawna behind me and disbelief flashed across his face. "What are you doing here?" he accused.

I turned to see Shawna and her wide eyes glanced back and forth between me and Liam. Liam saw the look and turned narrowed eyes on me.

"Did you kidnap her?" His voice hardened when he spoke his next question. "Where is Phi?"

I couldn't tell if that last question was aimed at me or Shawna. Either way there was no reason for him to ask it. I frowned in confusion and stepped toward him. He pointed a finger at me, halting my movement.

"Don't come closer, Templar. You don't want to know what will happen. Give me the girl and I might just let you live." Liam moved his finger to point at Shawna as he finished his order, indicating I should hand over Shawna to him.

My frown deepened and I glanced behind me, wondering if Shawna knew what was happening. She looked just as confused then her eyes widened in realization. She pointed to my hair and I touched it wondering why she was bringing that up suddenly. Was there something on it? Eww, was there blood? I reached my hand up and brought a piece of hair around only to see that it was not my hair.

I was an idiot.

I yanked off the blonde wig and turned to Liam, finally realizing he didn't recognize me because I was in disguise.

His glare turned to wide eyed disbelief. "Phi?"

I cringed. "Yeah?"

Liam stomped forward and crushed me in a hug. "I was so scared they hurt you." He pulled back and anger replaced concern. "Why are you here?"

I looked away, trying to find a plausible answer that wouldn't get me in trouble. "Well..." I stopped, unable to think of anything. Ugh, truth it is then. "I had a tip that there would be a meeting about the professional hunters, so I came in disguise."

Liam's hands on my arms tightened until I squeaked in pain. He let me go and ran a hand through his hair. His gaze drifted to Shawna. "Why is she here?"

"Umm..." Again, I tried thinking of an answer that wouldn't get us in trouble or her killed but came up with nothing.

Shawna stepped forward and pushed her shoulders back, bracing herself to say something difficult. "I am her informant."

Liam blinked at her. "Say what now?"

Shawna took a deep breath and let it out slowly. "I am a Templar."

Suddenly my arm was gripped in Liam's hand again while Shawna got the same treatment with his other. "We're leaving."

Liam dragged us to the door that I tried to go through earlier and nodded his head to it indicating for one of us to open it. I quickly put my knife away while Shawna reached out and did as he silently ordered.

Liam turned his head back to the fight and called out, "Let's go," but didn't wait for a response.

I expected someone to stop us but there was so much chaos that we were able to slip out unnoticed. Liam didn't wait for the others. Instead he guided Shawna and me forcefully out of the building then toward his house. When we were far enough away, I yanked on my arm. Liam refused to let go so I pinched him and used his surprise to get my arm free. Liam stopped abruptly and turned to me with fire in his eyes. We stood there, face to face, glaring and waiting for the other to crack first.

Kaden and Trevor trotted up to us, breaking up our standoff with their presence. Liam turned to them and roughly pushed Shawna at Kaden. I shouted and went to help her, but Trevor stepped in front of me blocking my attempt. I glared at him, but it had no effect.

We walked silently back to the house, all of us keeping an eye on our surroundings. How had the others escaped the room? Did they kill everyone? The thought frightened me but also kind of relieved me. I felt ashamed for feeling relieved, but it would mean my life wasn't in danger. I would have to ask them later about it since I doubted anyone wanted to talk at the moment. I kept glancing back to see if Shawna was okay and she would nod each time to reassure me, but I could tell by the way she was rubbing her arm that Liam probably left a bruise and the tears watering her eyes was because of Kaden's cold shoulder demeanor.

Liam waved us inside once we got to the house then checked the perimeter to make sure we were not followed. I immediately walked to the kitchen table knowing we would have a meeting even though I really wanted to run up to my room and hide in there forever. I could sneak up food later then switch to online classes, so I never had to leave the safety of my room. I would totally be fine. However, I knew I would have to face the guys some time and there was no way I would leave Shawna down here to explain all on her own. So, I pulled out a chair and plopped into it, bracing myself for the inevitable.

Shawna sat down next to me but kept her head bowed. Kaden and Trevor took the other two chairs which left Liam standing when he got back. He probably didn't mind though since he kept pacing and running his hand through his hair. I cringed at the state I put him in. I had never seen him so unhinged.

"Tell us *exactly* what happened," Liam ordered after coming to a stop at the table. He leaned over it with his hands on the table and looked between me and Shawna waiting for one of us to speak. Trickles of fear made their way into my mind and body. Shawna whimpered and that's when I knew Liam was using his talent.

I slapped my hand on the table, causing everyone to jump. "Quit it!"

The fear instantly vanished.

I leaned back in my chair and fidgeted with my bracelet. "I found out Shawna was a Templar, and long story short she ended up being one of the good ones so she has been giving me information and tonight there was a meeting so I went hoping to find out more about the professionals.”

The guys stared at me then slowly switched their focus to Shawna. Shawna suddenly jumped up and started yelling at us. “It was not my choice! I never wanted this life! Leave me alone!” I stared open mouthed at her outburst. What brought that on? I glanced at Kaden and watched as he tightened his fist and Shawna raged louder.

Gah! Why can’t these guys go one second without torturing Shawna? I stood up and reached out, slapping Kaden on the back of the head then sat back down. I pierced each of them with my best glare. “Leave her alone.”

Kaden shouted in surprise and rubbed his head as he frowned. At least he wasn’t making Shawna angry anymore. Shawna took deep breaths then sat down again. I noticed she scooted her chair back a little bit, not wanting to be attacked by their talents anymore.

“You guys can trust her,” I told them.

“What about you?” Liam asked.

I looked to him, startled. “What do you mean?”

“Every time I turn around you are doing something dangerous. Going to that meeting was the worst thing you could have done. You could have been killed! You’re lucky we were able to track your phone. How am I supposed to trust you?”

That hurt. "You wouldn't have let me go if I told you and you would have hurt her," I pointed to Shawna to emphasize my point, "if I told you about her identity."

"We wouldn't have hurt her," Kaden whispered.

Shawna's head snapped up at that, but Kaden refused to look at her. I didn't believe Kaden. He may not have hurt her, but Liam and Trevor would have if it meant keeping us safe. They were the hit-first-ask-questions-later type. Plus, wasn't Kaden the one affecting her with his talent not even two minutes ago?

"I would never hurt you guys," Shawna said addressing everyone but keeping her gaze on Kaden.

The guys didn't respond, and I didn't know if that meant they believed her or that they didn't and would be dealing with her later. Either way, it was not the most pressing issue that needed to be addressed. She was safe for now and I would protect her from the guys.

"Ok, so do you want to hear about what happened at the meeting?"

At their expectant stares I dove into the story then they made me repeat it two more times. Shawna added details that I missed and soon the guys knew everything we witnessed earlier that night. They tried to make us repeat it one more time, convinced we missed some details, but I refused. I was exhausted and I wasn't sure how many more angry glares I could take.

Liam frowned, ready to object but I held my hand up. "You guys, I need sleep. We all need sleep."

"Fine, we can pick this up tomorrow," Trevor jumped in for the first time. Liam finally nodded and we all stood to go our separate ways.

"I will walk her home," Trevor announced, noticing Liam and Kaden refused to look at Shawna.

I held out my hand to stop him. "No, she should stay here."

"Like hell she will," Liam burst out.

I sighed, feeling exasperated with him already but I understood he was only looking out for us. "Yes, she is in just as much danger as we are now that she revealed her loyalty to us at the meeting."

I expected them to refuse still and yell about it, but they actually looked thoughtful. Well, Kaden and Trevor did. Liam still looked like he was about to explode.

"I will be fine," Shawna said softly, laying her hand on my arm. She started to walk to the front door.

"No, stay here," Kaden called out shocking us all. "I will get you a pillow and blanket, you can sleep on the couch." Kaden walked away without waiting for a response.

"Only one night," Liam announced before following Kaden up the stairs.

"Phi?" I turned to Trevor waiting for him to continue. He spoke softly but held a note of disappointment. "What you did tonight was really stupid."

I deflated and looked down in shame. "I know." Then I looked up with hardened eyes and a small frown ready to defend myself. However, there was no need.

"But you gained useful information, so thanks, I guess." Trevor walked over to a cabinet and pulled out some crackers then made his way to his room.

It was nice to know that at least one person in that house accepted my actions as useful. Pleased, I waved to Shawna and told her to shout for me if they tried hurting her, then went up to my room. As tired as I was, there was still one person I needed to talk to before I could sleep.

"Owen?" I called out once I was alone in my room.

A light appeared in front of me then an almost transparent body. I smiled when Owen's form materialized, and I took a step forward to hug him before I remembered he was not corporeal.

"How goes it, little sis?" Owen greeted.

I snorted and rolled my eyes. "You're only older by three minutes."

Owen chuckled then leaned against the wall. He studied me with keen eyes then frowned with concern. "What's wrong?"

I had to choke back tears. I had missed him so much and here he was picking up on my emotions even when he was dead. I shook my head, both as answer to his question and to push down the burning in my eyes. "Nothing." I said when I could speak without choking on emotion. "It's been a long night."

"Tell me about it," he said. I stared at him wondering if he was truly wanting to hear about it. When he smiled encouragingly, I laid everything out.

I told him exactly what I told the guys, including how I disguised myself. When I finished, I couldn't tell what his thoughts were. He only stared at me, unmoving and with no emotion, like a statue. For a second, I thought we lost our connection like a phone loses connection and drops a call. Was that how the ghost world worked?

Then he sighed, looking weary. "Phi, that was the stupidest thing you could have done."

"Eh, what!" I said. I thought he would have been the one to defend me on this.

"Phi, I have told you to trust the Horsemen. You should have told them your plan and about your friend. What if something happened to you?"

I grumbled, knowing he was right but not wanting to admit it.

"Also, why didn't you summon me when you were there?"

I tilted my head in confusion. Why would I have summoned him at the meeting? What could a ghost do in that situation?

Understanding my head tilt, he explained, "I could have been your look out or helped discern things you couldn't."

"Huh, I didn't think of that," I admitted.

Owen shook his head and sighed. "At least you're okay, but don't do that next time without backup."

Hopefully there would not be a next time. I nodded, accepting his terms. See? I could be reasonable. That is, when I am not being yelled at.

My door creaked and I looked over to see Liam walking in. I tensed getting ready for another battle. Yes, what I did was stupid and yes, I can admit that I should have told them, but I would defend my actions no matter what.

"I will leave you guys to do…whatever it is you're about to do," Owen said then disappeared taking the ghostly light with him.

I turned around fully and crossed my arms, annoyed that Liam chased away Owen even if it wasn't intentional. "Why are you here?"

Liam frowned at me and crossed his arms then uncrossed them, then stuck a hand in his pocket and took it out a second later. I eyed Liam up and down wondering why he was so nervous. He swept a hand through his hair which had become a habit apparently. Finally finding his words he stepped forward and softly gripped my arms in his hands.

"You scared me today, High Phi."

I usually would have scolded him for using my given nickname but this time he said it endearingly. His admission sent a shock through me and I instantly felt guilty. The fight left my body and I lunged forward to hug him tight. He may overreact most times, but it all stemmed from love and feeling like he needed to protect everyone. I buried my face in his shirt and squeezed my eyes closed.

"I'm sorry. Next time I will include you."

Liam's chest rumbled. "There better not be a next time."

I couldn't promise that, but I could take my brother's advice and trust them with my plans, so I would include Liam if there came a next time. Liam pulled me away from him and I nearly pouted from being separated from his warmth.

Without any warning, Liam leaned into me and kissed me deeply. It felt different than the other kisses we shared. This one was hard and demanding. He was showing me how scared he had been and how relieved he was that I was okay. I kissed back just as fervently, showing him that I was sorry. I lost myself in the kiss and when he pulled back, I felt dizzy. My lips felt tender and swollen and a heat filled the space between us. I bit my lip feeling a little awkward and embarrassed by our display of emotion. His eyes traveled down to stare at my lips and his hand reached up to trace the lines of them. My breath caught at the intimate motion.

"Let me hold you tonight," Liam said softly and stepped closer to me.

I had to look up to see his face. "Um, I don't know about that." I didn't know if hold was code for something more, and I was definitely not ready for that.

Somehow reading my mind Liam's cheeks reddened. It was adorable to see the big, bad Horseman blushing. "No, not that, well unless you want to, but I just want to hold you in my arms so that I can reassure myself that you're okay."

I chuckled at his flustered state. "Mhm, if you say so." I walked over to the bed and got under the covers. Liam stood at the foot of the bed staring down at me, hope and hesitancy shining in his eyes. I patted the space beside me, and he took no time in reaching it.

He pulled me into his side and locked me in place with a strong arm. I felt his breath on the top of my head as he settled against me.

"I'm not going anywhere," I told him, trying to reassure him.

His chest rumbled against my back. "You better not."

I rolled my eyes at his bossiness but smiled and fell asleep against his warm chest.

Chapter 19

I convinced the guys to let Shawna stay all weekend and they grudgingly agreed. However, tension rose in the air once again when Monday rolled around. We all had to go to class, but the danger lurking somewhere outside kept us on edge as we prepared to leave. I slipped my pocketknife into my pocket, pepper spray into my inside jacket pocket, and couple of daggers in my backpack. I still felt vulnerable but at least I had been practicing my talent and could use that as my main defense.

Trevor chuckled at me on our way to our first class. I kept jumping at every sound and eyeing every person we passed. Apparently, my caution and paranoia were funny to him. I smacked him on his arm when I heard him snickering after I jumped at another sound, but that only made him chuckle louder. We made it on time to Math and it took everything I had to stay focused on the lesson. I kept expecting to be stabbed in the back by one of my classmates since I sat in the first row which left my back open to those behind me. Yet nothing happened. By English I began to breathe easier, especially when Liam and I sat in the back so we could keep our eyes on everyone. Kaden, Shawna and I met each other outside of class for Engineering Design so we could walk in together and watch each other's backs. The whole day passed by smoothly and I didn't know whether that was a good or bad thing. That night we walked Shawna to our dorm to grab a bag then moved her into the house until all this crazy passed. I could tell the guys still did not trust her. They watched her like a hawk and always kept their distance. I just hoped they would come to see that she was a good person like I had come to know.

We continued the routine every day until I finally started to relax. If they were going to attack us on campus during school hours, they would have done it by now. Feeling confident in my hypothesis I sauntered into Math on Wednesday the next week and took my seat. Trevor settled into the seat next to me and immediately slouched in his chair and pulled his hood up to take a nap until class started. There has been a chill in the air, hinting at the new season, so Trevor had taken to wearing a sweatshirt rather than his brown leather jacket. I rolled my eyes at him then doodled in my notebook while I waited for the teacher. I had come up with an amazing new engineering project that involved a pulley system and I couldn't help drawing it out in all my notebooks when I got the chance. I was just adding the wheels on the pulley in the corner of my page when the teacher walked in. I shook Trevor awake then proceeded to open his notebook for him, so it looked like he had been ready the whole time. Trevor had fallen asleep in class once before and got reprimanded so I was trying to prevent that from happening again. Trevor slammed his fist on the table causing me to sit back startled. I looked up at him, but he wasn't looking at me. His jaw was clenched, and his hands were balled into fists on the desk. I followed his line of sight and gasped when I saw what had him on edge.

John, the professional hunter, smirked at us knowing Trevor's outburst was about him. I reached for my pocketknife but stopped when I realized I wouldn't get far. This was a classroom and I could be arrested for attacking someone with a knife in school. Why was he there? John answered my question when he began putting math problems on the board. No freaking way.

John turned to the class and waved. "Hello, I will be subbing for Mr. Jackson until further notice. My name is Mr. Smith."

I made a derisive snort. John Smith? Really? That probably wasn't even his real name. Which made me wonder if Peter and Dean used their real names. Maybe they went by Peter Pan and Dean Winchester. I chuckled internally, amused at the thought.

John ignored Trevor and me as he taught his lesson, but Trevor and I never stopped glaring at him. I don't think either of us wrote down one note because we were so busy watching our enemy act as if he was an innocent professor. I could tell Trevor wanted to jump over his desk and charge John Smith, killing him right there, but that would cause a scene and knowing people of the 21st century it would be all over the internet in less than a second. I laid my hand on his arm to keep him from doing something irrational even though I wanted to do the same thing. I felt his tense muscles underneath his sweatshirt, but he relaxed a bit, seeming to understand what I wanted.

Class dismissed sometime later and we both darted to intercept the teacher before the next set of students arrived.

"What the hell do you think you're doing?" Trevor asked getting up close and personal with the professor. Trevor's chest bumped against John's threateningly, but John only smiled smugly.

"I'm preparing my lesson," John answered casually, as if Famine were not literally breathing down his neck.

I tried to pull Trevor back, but it was like moving a brick wall. I huffed in annoyance and leaned around him to see John better. I levelled him with one of my best glares. "Why are you teaching this class? Don't think you can throw us off guard. We're watching you."

John chuckled and shook his head. "As we are watching you," he said cryptically.

Trevor growled and looked like he was about to rip the hunter's head off. Sounds of shuffling footsteps and chatter from students coming into the room halted any attack either of them would have done. I gave Trevor's arm one last yank. Any second now the students would see that something was happening.

Thankfully Trevor realized the same thing and backed away. We both left the room, glancing behind us a few times to make sure John wouldn't run up and stab us right there. I left feeling confused and angry. After a week of nothing, they suddenly made a move and I didn't know how to feel about it. What did he mean they were watching us too?

I waved to Trevor as we parted ways and ran to my English class. We had spent too much time with John, and I was almost late. Good thing the buildings were close. I barged into the room and everyone stopped what they were doing to stare at me. I glanced at the front and thankfully we still had the same teacher as before except this time he was frowning at me. I mouthed sorry to him and walked to the back where Liam already sat saving a rolling desk-chair for me. As soon as I sat down, a piece of paper landed on my desk. I don't know why he continued to write notes when we both had phones, but elementary antics are his forte, I guess. I chuckled to myself, thinking about his mock outrage if he had heard me say that out loud. I waited for class to continue before I opened the note.

Way to make an entrance. Everything ok?

I grabbed my pencil and angrily relayed everything about John as my Math teacher and his ominous words. I tossed it to Liam and crossed my arms with a frown on my face. Liam tilted his head in confusion, wondering why I was mad, then opened the note to find the answer. Liam cursed quietly and looked up to search my face. I wasn't sure if he was looking for injuries or wondering if I was serious.

The door to the classroom opened again and everyone's heads swiveled to look at the person coming in. The teacher sighed and turned to the person coming in with an irritated look. Liam and I gasped when we saw who it was.

Dean.

I knew exactly what would happen, so I immediately placed my hand on Liam's arm to prevent him from launching himself at the Templar. Dean looked around the classroom and smirked when his eyes landed on us. He ignored the teacher's glare and sauntered to the back of the classroom and took a seat ten feet from where we sat. Liam struggled to stay calm. He clenched his fists and murmured murderous things about Dean. Dean continued smirking but never shot us another glance, just like John. What were they doing?

Their presence made me uneasy and paranoid that something would happen any second. Maybe their goal was to have a Horseman attack them, so they had 'no choice' but to 'defend' themselves. That was my best guess. I could tell Liam was not paying attention to the teacher because he kept glaring at Dean. I had trouble listening to the teacher too because I had to spend my whole time focused on keeping Liam from attacking Dean.

If every day was going to be like that then my grades were going to be in trouble. I couldn't afford to fail. As soon as class ended, I shuffled out of the building just as everyone else did but waited until Dean sauntered out to grab his wrist and pull him to the side of the building. Liam followed me, balling his fists, probably thinking we were about to hurt Dean, but I had something else in mind.

When I released Dean's wrist he leaned against the wall and smiled at us smugly. I really wanted to punch the smugness off his face, but I took a deep breath to curb that feeling.

"Ok, listen up dude. I don't know what you guys are planning, but it is going to mess with my schooling, and I can't have that. So why don't you run along and tell the Templars we are not a danger then leave us the hell alone." I smiled sweetly then waved and started to walk away.

"You *are* a danger!" Dean lunged at Liam with a knife and took a swipe at him.

Liam grabbed Dean's wrist and bent it until Dean dropped the weapon then punched him. Dean stumbled back from the blow but smiled. They circled each other with raised fists. I felt Liam push out his talent hoping to scare Dean so bad he couldn't fight back.

Dean smirked. "Nice try, but I have been trained to withstand fear, anger, and sickness. You can't affect me that easily." Dean shot out a fist which connected with Liam's side.

That was all Liam needed and soon they were rolling around trying to get the upper hand. I rolled my eyes. When Liam popped back up after hitting Dean in the face with his fist again, I jumped in between them. Dean didn't care though. He swung out trying to connect with my stomach but thankfully Kaden had trained me well. I stepped to the side then grabbed Dean's wrist as it missed its mark and pushed as much of my talent as I could without killing him.

"Have you been trained against loss?" I learned there was more to Death then just sickness. There was loss which could break any being. So, while Dean may have been trained against feeling sick, I figured feeling the despair and ache of loss would work.

I was right. Dean crumpled in on himself and cried out. Tears poured down his face and his other hand that was not held in mine clutched at his chest. I leaned down until I was near his ear and whispered. "This is what we feel every time you take one of us from each other. If you don't want to feel this every day of your life after we take one of yours, I suggest you stop hunting us."

With that, I released his hand and left him to get his bearings. Liam trailed after me and grabbed my shaking hand to offer comfort. I squeezed his hand, accepting the comfort and led us to my next class. I knew Liam didn't have a class until later, so he stayed with me until we reached the Engineering building where Kaden and Shawna waited. We quickly filled them in on the hunter's actions and warned them to expect the last one to show up sometime. Liam waved to us and left leaving the rest of us to go into our next class.

Seeing Peter up front next to our professor didn't even faze me. He was introduced as a grad assistant, but I tuned the rest out. Kaden was fuming and Shawna looked frightened but otherwise we ignored him. The three professionals had wormed their way into our schedules, but we would just have to wait and see what the purpose was.

As the days passed, we saw one or all of them everywhere we went rather than just in class. Whether it was at the cafeteria, a restaurant, the store, or around campus. They were stalking us, and it was creeping me the hell out. Thankfully the illness that had killed eight people stopped and no more bodies showed up with my symbol on their arm. I didn't know what to think about that and no one ever showed themselves to claim credit for framing me, so I had to demote it on my things-to-worry-about list.

It was a Thursday night when we decided to loosen up the tension by having another movie night. Shawna sat next to Kaden and Trevor on the couch like last time while Liam and I sat on the floor, with our backs against the legs of our roommates. The guys had warmed up to Shawna over the last couple of weeks and she had become like one of us. I was happy to see their acceptance of her because it was getting awkward how they would leave a room if she were in it. Now they included her in our meetings and camaraderie. Kaden had even started training her in self-defense.

We were at the part in Harry Potter when Professor Quirrell runs into the dining hall shouting about a troll. As soon as the professor collapsed in the movie a loud shattering noise sounded behind us making me and Shawna scream. I am pretty sure I heard Trevor scream too but he would never admit it. Kaden paused the movie and we turned around to find our living room window destroyed and glass all over the carpet.

"Be careful where you step," Liam advised as he made his way to the broken window.

I followed him and noticed a rock with a piece of paper rubber banded around it on the floor among the broken glass. I picked my way across the floor to retrieve it then slipped the piece of paper off the rock.

"What is that?" Shawna asked, noticing my attention was on something other than glass.

The guys looked over at Shawna's words, so I read the note out loud. "Watch your backs." I huffed in annoyance. "Really? This is just harassment now."

Liam looked pissed. He grabbed the rock from me and tossed it out of the broken window. "Kaden grab something to put over this, Trevor call a repair man, girls pick up the glass. Then we are all going to have a meeting. This shit needs to end now!"

Kaden and Trevor rushed away to get their part done. Shawna and I grabbed the trash can and began picking up pieces of broken glass. When everyone was finished, we met at the kitchen table. I poured us all a glass of lemonade and fidgeted with my glass as we waited for someone to start the conversation. I knew they were going to say something like kill them and get rid of the bodies, but I really didn't want to do that. However, the professional hunters were endangering and threatening us, so something needed to be done.

"I am honestly surprised they didn't do anything sooner," Shawna stated, breaking the angry silence.

Liam's dark gaze landed on Shawna, making her squirm. "Do you know what they might do next?"

Shawna shook her head. "I've never really been involved in Templar stuff, so I don't know. I'm sorry."

We all sighed with disappointment.

"Well, we need to figure out what they will do next otherwise one of us might get hurt next time," Trevor said.

"It's not like we can ask them," Kaden grumbles.

I sat up straighter as an idea made its way into my mind. I tapped the glass of lemonade in my hand with my fingernail as I sorted through the idea then slapped the table once I got it causing their attention to land on me. "Maybe we *can* ask them."

Trevor and Kaden snorted in disbelief and Shawna shook her head sadly. Only Liam looked curious.

"What is that pretty little head thinking?" Liam asked, causing a blush to burn my cheeks.

I shook my head to rid myself of the fluttery feelings and focused on the problem. "Well, we could kidnap one of them and ask him what their plan is. They have been antagonizing us so we will only be giving them what they want. And if asking them about their plan doesn't work then it will at least draw the others here so we can end it once and for all. We have weapons and booby traps set up." I looked between the three guys waiting to see their reaction to my plan.

The guys looked at each other and seemed to have a silent conversation.

"You guys have booby traps?" Shawna asked wide eyed and looked around trying to see if she could spot any. I ignored her and kept my eyes on the guys.

All three Horsemen turned to me at once with wide grins. "Let's do it."

Chapter 20

I figured Dean would be the easiest to kidnap. John was a professor, and Peter was a grad student so they would be noticeable if they went missing. We put our plan into motion the next day. I handed over the chloroform and a rag to Trevor since it was his job to use it on the Templar. He and Kaden stood outside the English building and would intercept Dean on the way out of class. It was Shawna's duty to create a distraction and my job to be the look out when they carried Dean away.

It sounded so simple when laid out, but I knew from movies and books that the best laid out plans always went wrong somewhere. I just hoped it worked long enough to get him to our house.

Liam and I sat through class and watched Dean out of the corner of our eyes. The Templar sat there without a care in the world and it bugged me. How could he be so calm? Liam wanted to bring the note that the assailant threw through our window last night to shove in Dean's face, but I talked him out of it. We had plenty of time later for that if our plan went accordingly.

Once again, I had difficulty paying attention to the teacher. Man, I had become a terrible student but hopefully after today I would be able to focus on my studies again. There were only a few more weeks until finals and I still needed to do my final projects. It felt like forever before the teacher finally called the end to class. Knowing Dean would wait for us to leave before he did, we had picked up on that habit earlier that week, we waited for the other students to trickle out so there would be less witnesses outside.

Liam and I acted as if we were ignoring Dean and walked out together, holding hands and whispering to each other. Occasionally I threw in a small giggle as if he was flirting, but really, we were readying ourselves for what we had to do next. Outside, students shuffled in and out of the building as they all rushed to their next class. Liam and I glanced back to see if Dean was watching then sprinted to the side of the building. What I was betting on was that the hunters were keeping a close eye on us and that Dean would be curious as to why we deviated from our usual route. Honestly, I was banking on curiosity killing the cat, or in this case, the Templar.

We rounded the corner and met Trevor and Kaden. As soon as they saw us, they soaked the rag with chloroform and put their backs against the wall. I almost squealed with glee when Dean rounded the corner not even a minute later. Liam immediately punched Dean which sent the Templar reeling back. Kaden wrapped his arms around him while Trevor pressed the rag against Dean's nose and mouth. Dean struggled and kicked trying to get free, but they held him tight. I peeked around the corner to make sure we were not seen and saw Shawna's distraction playing out.

Fireworks exploded on the other side of the building and led down the walkway away from us. Students clapped and cheered and followed the line of fireworks to see more. I wanted to go see the sparks and exploding colors too but there were more pressing matters. I turned back to the guys and saw Trevor putting his hoodie on Dean then propping the Templar up between him and Kaden. Liam walked in front of them to hide the body with his tall frame. I fell to the back of the group to hide him from direct view although my frame would not cover him completely which is why Shawna fell into step beside me once we walked away from the English building. To anyone else it would look like a group of people walking by with their arms around each other. Maybe a little drunk.

Thanks to the fireworks that continued its display we were able to get Dean away from the area and to our house with almost no one noticing. I saw a few people look our way curiously, but no one stopped us or looked too closely. I honestly expected someone to shout at us to stop or to call the police, but it was strangely easy to kidnap this Templar which made me concerned about the university's security and safety of their students.

Before we left that morning, we set up a chair with rope in the kitchen because it didn't have any windows and had only one point of access. As soon as we got into the house, we placed Dean in the chair and tied him around the chest to the back of the chair then tied his hands and feet. I had to admit, rope was better than sheets. I glanced at Shawna wondering if this brought up memories of when I tied her to a chair. She didn't meet my eyes so I couldn't tell what she thought. Kaden searched him for weapons and pulled a couple of knives from his person. Now all we had to do was wait. A couple of us did our homework at the table to keep an eye on Dean while the others gathered weapons and planned for when the others arrived. I heard Dean's phone buzz every so often and pulled it out of his pocket to see who was messaging him. John and Peter's name appeared multiple times as they sent him texts. It was only a matter of time before they figured it out. I wondered if they had a tracking app on each other's phones.

I took a break from homework to make us all some lunch when I heard a groan come from the direction of the chair that Dean was tied to. I quickly called for the others. They arrived just as Dean looked around trying to figure out where he was and what happened. As soon as he saw us, he narrowed his eyes and started cursing. His eyes landed on Shawna last and he cursed even more and called her a traitor. I rolled my eyes and stepped in front of Shawna, blocking his view of her.

"What do you think you're doing?" Dean spat when his cursing died down. "You know they're going to come for me, right?"

"Counting on it," Liam said, and Dean's eyes widened as he realized our plan. Liam held up the note that crashed through our window last night. "You went too far with this. We don't take well to threats."

Dean scrunched his eyebrows at it then at each of us. "We didn't do that. We are not so juvenile."

"Says the person harassing us by stalking us," Trevor grumbled.

Dean gave us a smug smile. "Oh, trust me, if we wanted to threaten you it would have been much worse than a note."

Liam raised his fist and punched Dean causing his head to spin to the side and blood to spatter from his mouth.

"Liam!" I admonished.

Liam only rolled his eyes. "They will be here eventually, there is no need to talk to him." Then he walked away followed by Kaden and Shawna.

Trevor and I stayed in the kitchen to watch him. I continued with my sandwich making while Trevor munched on carrots. I really wanted to ask Dean about how he got involved with the Templars and what their plans were for us. I doubted Dean would tell us about their plans, seeing as he was a "professional", so I just stayed quiet.

Apparently, Dean didn't have the same desire for silence. "You guys are making a mistake. They will kill you. I will too when I am free."

Trevor and I continued our silence. We were not too concerned. With my booby traps, our fighting skills, and our powers there was no way three Templars could survive.

"You deserve to be brought down for what you have done."

That got my attention. I marched over to stand in front of Dean with a sandwich in one hand. "And what do you think it is we've done?"

"You in particular should die a most gruesome death for spreading a disease and killing innocents. As for the others, it is only a matter of time before they start something too." Dean stared at me with hatred and disgust shining in his eyes.

I gaped at him and looked over his head to give Trevor an *is this guy serious* look. I looked back to Dean when Trevor shrugged.

"For a professional, you are really stupid," I said and bit into my sandwich. Anger boiled underneath my skin, but I stood there proud for keeping my voice calm.

Dean's hate filled eyes and frown faltered for a second then he shook his head in disbelief. "We all know it was you, spreading your pestilence and trying to start the apocalypse."

I stared at him for a second then started laughing. Deep howling laughter that I couldn't stop if I tried and tears made their way down my cheeks. Trevor chuckled a bit at the table, but I didn't know if he found Dean's statement humorous too or if he was reacting to my mirth.

When my laughter finally subsided and I caught my breath, I waved a hand in the air and said, with laughter still in my voice, "Whew, that was a good one. I haven't laughed like that in a long time. Thanks." I took a large bite of my sandwich.

Dean's expression was more puzzled than angry now, although there were still hints of that in his eyes. I didn't wait for him to ask about the laughter.

"Dean, I would never, ever, hurt someone on purpose, especially with pestilence. And there is no way I would start the apocalypse. I love this world too much. The other guys wouldn't either. We all just want to be left alone. It is you guys who keep starting things by attacking us and triggering our defense mechanisms."

In a way I was telling the truth. I doubted the guys' talents worked like defense mechanisms, but my pestilence talent triggered when I was attacked and felt defenseless. I had come a long way in controlling it, but I couldn't help it if I was only defending myself.

Dean snorted. "You're lying."

I shrugged showing him I didn't care about his opinion. "Just think about this. When has a victim of the Horseman Death or Pestilence been marked by a scythe symbol? And if we were the terrible beings you think us to be, then why are you still alive?"

I didn't wait to hear his words. I walked away to the living room, needing to get away from the Templar before I slapped him with the sandwich I held. His words bothered me, and I hated that anyone would think so terribly of me. I was not a monster, but they obviously deemed me one just because I happened to be Death. I never chose this life, and the guys were born into it. It sucked that the stories made us out to be evil. I just wanted to graduate college and become an engineer. Forget the apocalypse. I was starting to think the near-end-of-the-world moments in the past were caused by Templars messing with things they shouldn't. The worst part was the Templars thought they were doing the right thing. It was their holy mission to destroy the bringers of the apocalypse. Well they should destroy themselves then. I angrily bit into my sandwich, attempting to take out my frustrations on the food.

Trevor called us all to the kitchen a couple hours later where he held Dean's phone up in the air. It buzzed continuously indicating a call rather than a text. Liam stepped forward and grabbed the phone, answering it then putting it on speaker. I glanced at Dean wondering what he would do. Was he going to warn them away? Call for help? I doubted he would show that kind of weakness, so my guess was the former one.

"Dean, you missed check in," John's voice said through the phone.

Liam stared at Dean, daring him to say something as he answered, "That's unfortunate. Maybe you should do something about it."

Dean stayed quiet but eyed Liam carefully.

A moment of pause then, "Who is this?" John asked.

"Guess. You have 24 hours." Then Liam hung up and smiled. "Well that should motivate them." The other guys chuckled but Dean shook his head.

"You're making a mis-" Dean started to say.

I waved his words away and interrupted, "Bla, bla, bla. We've already done this routine." I turned to the guys. "Let's get ready."

The first trap outside sprung, starting with a snap of a twig, a curse from whoever triggered it, then an air horn alerting us to the presence of the incoming threat. I stood by the broken window with Liam, while Kaden and Trevor stood by the door. We gave Shawna a knife and sent her to the kitchen as the last defense. Kaden had been training her, but her skills were still weak. The first set of people crashed through the front door and chaos erupted. Shawna warned us that John and Peter would most likely bring more Templars with them, especially after our show of strength at their meeting. Looks like she was right. The second trap near the front door sprung sending nails raining down and the first set of people cried out in pain. My traps were meant to be alarms and to cause injury not death, but I cringed all the same when I heard the nails clatter against flesh and the floor.

I didn't have time to ask if Kaden and Trevor were okay because a new set of people made their way into the house through the broken window. My third trap sprung, and pepper spray sprayed all over the incoming Templars causing them to scream and stumble around. Those that did not fall back out were knocked unconscious by the butt of our weapons while they were disoriented. The last trap was near the kitchen and had not sprung yet, so it was time to fight.

Ten more people made their way through the window, stepping passed those that were affected by the pepper spray. I didn't get to find out how many came through the door because the first blade swung toward my head and I barely deflected it in time. I chose my scythe to fight with since this was the only time I could carry it without people giving me a weird look. I also thought Death carrying a scythe would strike fear into some Templars, giving me an advantage in the fight.

I was wrong.

It only made them angrier.

Two more blades, one shorter than the other, swung at me, one aiming for my head and the other wilder, not caring where it landed as long as it did. I hooked the curved blade of my weapon around the wild short blade and tossed it to the side, throwing the guy's swing off. Then I brought around the pole at the end of the scythe to intercept the sword. I expected the sword to slice through the pole, seeing as how my weapon was, like, two thousand years old, whereas that dude's sword looked newer. But my weapon held strong and I was able to push him back. I brought the pole end up and smashed it into the two Templar's faces, rendering them unconscious.

More Templars and weapons came at me, but I continued my defensive and offensive moves, feeling like a total ninja warrior at how expertly I wielded the ancient weapon while spinning around my opponents. Kaden taught me well.

Liam knocked a few around as well but instead of using his Horsemen weapon, a bow and arrow, he used a common sword which he wielded expertly. Between the both of us we managed to reduce the numbers coming in through the window and we hadn't even pulled out our Horsemen gifts yet. A blonde head appeared briefly in the crowd, but I lost it among the fight. For some reason it had caught my attention and I had the urge to hunt it down. A fist clocked me in the chin, drawing my eyes back to the fight at hand and away from the familiar blonde head.

"Ow! That hurt!" I shouted as I rubbed my jaw.

Another fist rushed at me, but I leaned back, avoiding it by a centimeter. My fist came up reactively and connected with someone's mouth. I hissed at the pain that now radiated up my arm. The guy across from me laughed at my pain and spit blood from his injured mouth on our floor. I gaped at him in disgust.

"What the hell? That's rude," I scolded then punched him again, making him slump onto the spit on the floor.

Our area was cleared out for the most part, so I made my way out of the living area to help Shawna defend her spot. I cursed when I saw her at knife point and rushed over to help. Why did the booby trap not work?

"One step closer and I slit her throat," the blonde-haired Templar threatened. I recognized him as the brother of the movie theater Templar and as the one who attacked me in the library.

I stopped and glanced at Dean who eyed the whole thing from his seat. No one had gotten to him yet to untie him, but I kept him in my sights all the same. I risked a glance back, but the guys were still holding off the other Templars. John and Peter could be seen at the front. They were holding their own successfully, but I knew Trevor and Kaden could handle themselves.

"Let her go," I said, turning back to the Templar holding Shawna and slowly put my scythe down on the floor to show him I was not going to hurt him. Even though my body screamed for me to jump forward and smash my fist into his stupid face.

"She's a traitor and deserves to die with the rest of you," he said, with barely contained disgust.

My heart jumped at his words. Did that mean he was going to kill her no matter what? My friend's eyes were wide with terror. She gripped the arm holding the knife to her neck, trying to pry the hand away. I shook my head slightly, trying to tell her not to fight back or he would kill her. I held up my hands placatingly, hoping if he focused on me, he would forget about Shawna.

"Hey, you're the one who attacked me first in that library."

That moment seemed so long ago. I was just an innocent college student who had been attacked by a crazy sword wielding maniac. That was the night I found out I was a Horseman. I was attacked again in a movie theater and harassed when I tried getting a smoothie. Yes, I still had a grudge about my smoothie.

"Actually, you and your sister are the ones who caused all this. If you both hadn't attacked me, I would be none the wiser about any of it." I waved my hands around to encompass all the Horsemen and Templar stuff.

The blonde-haired boy roared, causing me to jump back in an alarm. "Don't talk about my sister!" His face reddened until he looked like he would explode and his knife holding hand shook. Shawna pressed as far back as she could to avoid the knife, but a thin line of red on her neck told me she didn't succeed.

My heart raced. I couldn't lose someone else. Shawna may have lied to me about who she was, but she has more than made up for it. She was my roommate and my friend. I took a step forward and tried to appeal to him. "You don't want to be a murderer. Templars are all about saving humans not killing them. Let Shawna go. This is between you and me."

"It wouldn't be the first time," he said, shaking Shawna to show he wouldn't let her go.

I took another step forward, my hands still held up in a defensive gesture. "What do you mean?"

I had a niggling feeling I knew what he meant but I wanted him to say it out loud. He was so agitated and focused on me I bet he forgot Dean was sitting there. My hope was the blonde guy would hang himself with his words.

The Templar scowled at me. "You killed her," his voice cracked at the end with grief. "And no one would do anything about it!"

His hold on Shawna loosened as he fought tears and the ache growing in his chest. I could feel his pain and despair, his anger and grief. They all mixed to form the familiar feeling of loss. It was strange to feel it when it was not my own. In a way I understood how the Templar felt. I was the one who killed his sister and, in his eyes, I deserved to die. I would have been the same way if I met whoever had a hand in my brother's murder.

"So, I set you up by causing an epidemic and placing your mark on the dead. That way, the Order would have no choice but to kill you." He laughed and shook his head. "Worked like a charm." He was going slightly mad now and my concern for Shawna grew.

I gasped at his confession. Man, that was easier than I thought it would be. I glanced at Dean over my shoulder to see if he heard. He looked disappointed but resigned and nodded that he heard. I didn't know if that meant he would call off the attack on me or that he would deal with both of us now. The blonde Templar gave off a loud, pained, screeching noise causing my head to snap back around to him. He was holding his nose and the knife hand had loosened significantly. I noticed Shawna wincing in pain and holding the back of her head. I smiled, knowing she had just headbutted the man holding her hostage. I leapt forward the rest of the way and snatched Shawna away, pushing her behind me so the Templar only faced me.

When he took his hand away, I could see his nose was already turning purple. He looked pissed and I readied my talent just in case he did something drastic. This guy was not just fighting because he was told to do it. He was out for vengeance which meant I would need everything in my arsenal to survive.

"I am tired of waiting for them to act. If they won't do it, then I will." He lunged for me, his knife held out in front of him.

I used my foot to kick up my scythe from the floor, expecting to catch it midair like a badass. Instead I ended up kicking it across the floor, making him stumble slightly. Now the scythe was farther from me and his knife stayed on its trajectory to my chest. I backed up until my butt hit the kitchen table, preventing me from continuing my backpedaling. His blade came down, but I grabbed his wrist to stop its motion. He pushed his weight on me causing the blade to come down inch by inch. I stared at its sharp point with wide eyes. I used Kaden's training and kicked at his shin then dove to the side letting the momentum bring him down. He cursed and spun with me before he hit the table. He swung out again, but I was already moving away. I elbowed him in the face and kicked at his knee.

I hissed at a sudden sting in my arm. The Templar smirked at me and the red dripping from the cut on my body. I pushed through the pain and attacked him, this time adding some of my talent. Every time I managed to touch him, I pushed a little sickness and grief into him. It wasn't too hard to affect him since his emotions were heightened already. After each touch, he cried out and tears leaked from his eyes, but he wouldn't give up. He got another slice in, this one on my leg. I stumbled back and struggled to stand. It stung so badly.

He kicked out at my injured leg, connecting with the cut. I cried out and fell to my knee. He towered over me, a sick glint in his eye as if this was more than just vengeance. He was going to enjoy killing me. He raised his weapon and brought it down with force and a smile. On instinct I reached out and latched on to his leg, the closest point of contact I could reach. I pushed all my fear, anger, and despair into him then closed my eyes waiting for the impact. After a minute of no pain, other than from the cut in my arm and leg, I cracked my eyes open to see what happened. The Templar's knife was frozen a few inches from my chest. I looked up to see what had caused him to stop and black boils surrounded wide blue eyes and a rounded mouth that had opened in surprise. Black spots also dotted his hand and traveled up his arm. The Templar folded in on himself and collapsed, clutching at his stomach and writhing in pain. I stood quickly and backed away. My foot bumped into something and I looked down to see my scythe. I picked it up and held it in a defensive position, watching the Templar die slowly from whatever pestilence I inflicted upon him.

He attacked me and nearly killed me twice. I was only defending myself, but I still hated to see what my talent could do. It was sickening and heart wrenching. Something no one should ever experience, but here I was having inflicted it three times. It made my heart ache for their lost lives. Eventually the Templar stilled, and I finally glanced away. I hadn't noticed how quiet the house was until the pained groans from the Templar I fought ceased. Now that he was dead, I noticed no one was fighting anymore. Shawna stood near Dean with a knife pointed at him while she stared down John and Peter, the only Templars left standing. Liam, Trevor, and Kaden switched their focus from me to the Templars and back again. I stepped toward Dean to untie him, but John and Peter jumped in my way, holding up their own weapons.

I sighed, not ready for another battle. "I am not going to hurt him."

"Could have fooled us," Peter said calmly. Despite his calm voice I could tell from his tense muscles that he didn't trust us, and he would kill us if anyone made a move.

I looked over his shoulder at Shawna. "Untie him."

Kaden, Trevor, and Liam shouted objections, but I held up my hand silencing them. Shawna looked at Liam hesitantly then me. I nodded to let her know I was serious then spoke to John, the leader of their crew. "If we wanted to hurt him, he would be dead by now."

John didn't reply, instead he turned slightly to help Shawna untie Dean while Peter kept an eye on us all. I continued speaking, hoping to convince them of our innocence, despite the dead body in the middle of our kitchen.

"Look at him," I said pointing to the dead Templar. I grimaced at the black boils on his skin then looked at Peter. "This is how my Pestilence kills people. And no scythe mark left behind. Those other students were killed by him." I pointed to the Templar again to show Peter who was to blame.

"You guys think you are so good and doing what is right for humanity by killing the harbingers of the apocalypse," I put air quotes around the last words then pointed accusingly at the dead body again. "When really it was you guys hurting humanity."

"That was not us," Peter scoffed.

"Wasn't me either, yet you are about to try and kill us either way," I said, crossing my arms.

Liam came to stand beside me and put an arm over my shoulders, pulling me into his side. I relaxed a little, knowing he and my friends were there to fight with me and defend what was right.

"What makes you think we would believe you?" John asked as if he didn't care about a single thing I said. He helped Dean stand up and Shawna quickly went to stand by Kaden, getting far from the professionals before she was used as a hostage again.

I heard groans and shuffling from the other rooms and shifted with worry. The other Templars were waking up and would be there soon to help the professionals in round two. I didn't think I could last another round.

"She's telling the truth," Dean announced. He rubbed at his wrists where the rope had secured them. "I heard him admit it."

He stood between John and Peter and spared a brief glance at the fallen Templar before bringing his eyes to rest on me. "Even though you did not cause this epidemic why should we believe you won't do something later on?"

Templars began to appear on the edges of the kitchen, watching what was going down between us and their superiors. If I had to fight again, I would have to rely on my Talent and I definitely did not want to kill any more people. I knew Liam, Trevor, and Kaden would do so if it meant protecting us. I sighed and pinched the bridge of my nose, trying to think of some way for us to get out of this.

"How about this?" I started. When I had their attention including the other Templars' I continued. "If a war, or famine, or epidemic happens and only if it was caused by us, then you can go ahead and kill us."

Kaden choked on air and coughed, surprised by my willingness to be killed. Trevor patted him on the back, trying to help him breathe easier. Liam smirked and squeezed my shoulder, letting me know he approved.

Peter snorted. "We could kill you right now and make sure that never happens."

Liam snorted back. "You could try." Then he sent a wave of fear over everyone. Not enough to send them screaming or to attack. Just enough to show them his power and warn them away from doing anything they might regret. "Conquest is not so easily killed."

"Is that a challenge?" Peter asked, narrowing his eyes and smiling.

Liam smirked. "One that you will lose."

I smacked Liam's arm and told him to quit provoking them. He chuckled but backed off.

"This is how this is going to go," I told them with authority. "You will all leave and if even one of you tries to attack us again, I will kill you." I stepped aside so the others could see the body in our kitchen then I copied Liam's tactic and sent a wave of my power over them, letting them feel what Death was all about. Some of the Templars backed away, fear shining in their eyes.

Dean was the one to speak up for everyone surprising both me and John. "Agreed. The Templars will leave you alone unless there is cause for us to intervene."

"Dean," John scolded softly, obviously opposed to making a pact with the four Horsemen.

I didn't wait for them to change their mind. "Good, now get your fallen and leave."

Each of us sent a wave of our talent over the Templars and professionals, showing them what was in store if they broke the deal. Fear, anger, despair, grief. Any of those could destroy a person.

They eyed each one of us, finally realizing whose company they stood in. We were the Four Horsemen. Conquest, War, Famine, and Death.

They rushed to grab their fallen and leave. John, Peter, and Dean paused at the door, looking back at us warily. The four of us stood together with one of their own showing them exactly who we were. Not the bringers of the apocalypse. Just five people who were thrown into unwanted roles and refused to let a prophecy define them. The Templars gave us a single nod then left, finally leaving us in peace.

Epilogue

I banged on the door loudly. "Let's go! You're the one who said you wanted to be there!"

Silence.

I beat at the door again, wanting him to wake up so we could go. Liam and Trevor were already waiting downstairs.

Giving up on the knocking I opened the door and barged in. Kaden had always told me I was welcome in his room, as long as I knocked first, so I didn't think it was a big deal.

Wrong. So wrong.

It was a very big deal.

Maybe not to him but to me it was. "My eyes!" I screeched in mock pain.

I held my hand up to cover the scene, backed out of the room, and closed the door to let them have their privacy. Well, good to know Kaden had forgiven Shawna. I shook my head trying to get the image of their naked bodies from my mind. They were not doing anything… you know, but they were cuddled up and naked and that was already more than I needed to see.

"Meet us downstairs!" I shouted through the door, then made my way down.

I saw Liam's questioning gaze when I came down the stairs, but I only shuddered in response. He chuckled and wrapped me in his arms. I melted against him and let him hold me.

"Are you sure about this?" Liam asked against my hair.

I nodded against his chest. "You all did it. It's my turn."

A few minutes later, Kaden came waltzing down the stairs beaming at us with Shawna in tow. Shawna chuckled and patted me on the back when she reached us. "Girl, I told you Kaden and I were inevitable."

"Inevitable, huh?" Kaden said with a sultry tone and wrapped his arms around her from behind.

I ignored her comment and glared at Kaden. "I will never go into your room again." We both knew that was a lie. He had too many books for me to ignore. But it would be a long while before I went in there on my own.

"Alright, stop wasting time or she will miss her appointment," Trevor reminded us.

We shuffled out of the house to the motorcycles. Eventually I would get one of those too, but for now my pale bicycle with a basket was good enough. I tied my black hair with its two white streaks behind my head then climbed onto the back of Liam's white motorcycle while Shawna rode on the red one with Kaden. Trevor put on his dark sunglasses and led us to my appointment with his black motorcycle.

We pulled up in front of the tattoo parlor and that's when the nerves hit me. I fidgeted with my Hawaiian bracelet and let Liam guide me inside. My stomach twisted in knots and my legs shook. I heard getting a tattoo hurt and I wondered if the sight of the needle would make me turn tail and run. I scolded myself internally. I dealt with sword wielders, knife attacks, crazy cultists, and Kaden as my trainer. I think I could handle a needle.

Trevor checked me in, and I was led into a curtained off area where a man with a thousand tattoos resided. I nodded my head in greeting and he guided me to sit in the dentist-like chair in front of him.

"So, I remember you saying over the phone you wanted this right?" He showed me a hand drawn picture next to him.

I nodded, flurries of excitement driving away the nerves. "Right here," I said pointing to the inside of my forearm. He took my arm and positioned it in front of him, palm facing up. Then he began cleaning the preferred area.

I looked around at all my friends lending me support but frowned. There was someone missing. As quietly as I could I summoned Owen and watched as his light materialized next to Liam. We were officially the start of a bad joke. Four Horsemen, a ghost, and a Templar walk into a tattoo parlor. I chuckled at the thought.

Owen smiled and his quiet support nearly made me cry. All these people together were more than I could have ever asked for. Liam glanced at Owen with unseeing eyes then at me with raised eyebrows. He knew Owen was there but couldn't see him. I nodded to let him know he was correct then focused back on the man with the needle.

I don't know how long we all waited quietly and watched the artist do his work but eventually the man sat back and put the needle away. "There you go. Take your pictures if that's what you want to do then I will bandage it."

The others crowded around me to admire the tattoo. Liam raised his sleeve to show me his bow and arrow on his bicep. Kaden lifted his shirt to show me the image of a sword on his abs. Trevor revealed his bicep and the scales adorning it. I looked at Owen and we both put our forearms next to each other to show off our identical tattoos of a scythe. The differences were that mine had the date Owen died below it and his glowed with a ghostly light. He gave me a smile tinged with sadness. I reciprocated it then looked over all my friends with content. I was no longer frightened by our future. We embraced who we were but didn't let it own us. Together we could get through anything.

Note from the Author

Ways to help Independent authors (without paying anything!):

--Rate and review the book on Amazon and Goodreads

--Follow them on social networks

--Post about the book

--Recommend to friends, family, and even strangers.

Your support means everything and would be much appreciated.

Acknowledgements

These past few months have been difficult, but I did it. First acknowledgement is to me for completing yet another story despite everything that has been going on and for continuing this book even when other people told me to focus on a different one. This story was fun to write.

Thank you to Harrison Lambeth for keeping me motivated and taking my kindle until I finished the necessary chapters.

Thank you, Victoria Gillette as always for being the one person to be there at the end to read and review so that my books are not embarrassingly riddled with errors. Thank you for also willingly talking to me about the story and characters.

A huge thank you to Jervy Bonifacio of Phoenix Design Studio from 99Designs who designed Myth Blessed and now Four Horsemen.

About the Author

Katie Dunn grew up in the hot part of Arizona where she graduated NAU and became a teacher. She got a taste of the author life after her first YA contemporary fantasy novel Ancient Elements. Finding out she loved writing just as much as reading, teaching, and traveling, she sat down and wrote the first installment of the YA fantasy adventure Skor Stone trilogy: Pirates from Under and YA contemporary fantasy novel Myth Blessed. She has a notebook full of other ideas and will slowly be adding more stories to her author library.

You can check out more about Katie Dunn's books and works in progress at Facebook.com/AuthorKatieDunn/ or Kdunnauthor.com

9 789898 524681 0